THE DREAM LIFE

"For a dreamer is one who can only find his way by moonlight, and his punishment is that he sees the dawn before the rest of the world."

-Oscar Wilde

GENE ROMAN

For R.L.S.& E.J.D.

and everyone who dares to dream.

For information, contact :
generomanbooks@gmail.com
generomanbooks.com

Book and Cover design by Gene Roman Books
ISBN: 979-8-218-82893-6
Book Formatting: Derek Murphy @Creativindie
Editing: Dr. Neal Blaxberg @ Your Pro Writer
Photography: Kristien King @blackgirlwaisted.com
First Edition: November 2025

Contents

CHAPTER 1

"Dream a little dream..."

"**M**ay we have your attention. Due to severe weather conditions, all departing flights at Hartfield-Jackson International Airport have been grounded until further notice. We will announce updates as soon as we receive information. We apologize for any inconvenience this may cause your travel plans. Thank you for choosing Delta as your premier mode of air transportation."

***

Even though it was obvious that the grounding announcement was destined to come due to the terrible weather conditions, I was praying that my flight would have already descended into the clouds beforehand.

"Great. Now I must inform LC that I won't be able to do the shoot today." I sighed heavily as I took out my phone to send my boss a travel update via text, because I didn't want to hear her demanding that I find a way to get there for the photoshoot, regardless of the storm. My flight was supposed to leave at 1:40 p.m. and arrive in New York at 3:30 p.m. The Elle photoshoot was set to begin at 5 p.m. in Harlem. I gazed out the window at the gloomy cumulonimbus clouds. The lightning strikes were hitting back-to-back. My phone rang.

"Hello, LC," I said instinctively, knowing it was her. Without a proper greeting, she ripped into me.

"Rae, you need to find a way to get your ass here ASAP. We don't do no-shows when my name is the frontrunner, especially for an Elle campaign, and you of all people know that!"

"Okay, let me just stop the thunderstorm that's going on in the sky, or I could hijack a plane and fly it myself. Which do you suggest?" I sarcastically remarked.

"You can be a smart ass all you want, but you need to find a way to get your butt here now! You are my most trusted first shooter, and this campaign needs your expertise to be done the right way. We can't let a little storm stop our money train."

I grew silent as I saw what was developing out in the distance.

"Hey, kid, are you there? You can't let me down. Hello. Say something…"

I couldn't respond because I was in awe of what I was witnessing. Not one, not two, but three twisters funnelled down from the deadly clouds and seemed to be heading directly toward the airport. I had never before seen such majestic weather happening right in front of my eyes. The announcements from the gate agent grew silent. I knew I should have been moving away from all the surrounding windows, but I couldn't look away from the ferocity and speed of the twisters headed in my direction. Time seemed to slow down as I turned to run for cover.

Suddenly, I realized I was the only one standing at the gate. The entire terminal suddenly went dark. A few seconds later, the generator re-lit the darkened space. Emergency lights flashed, and a blaring emergency recording repeated over and over. I looked back to see the twisters closing in. I wondered what had happened to all the people who had crowded the boarding gates just moments ago. The sound of a freight train passing grew louder and louder. As I slowly made my way toward the train that would take me to my gate, I could hear cries and prayers coming from people seeking cover. No sooner had I stepped onto the train than an unsettling wave of shattering glass hit my ears, and everything went black. I dropped to my knees and covered my head with my forearms, just like they taught us in grade school. A light, sky-like feeling washed over me, and what sounded like hail began pounding on my head. I glanced up, and sure enough, it was hail. About two inches of tiny ice pebbles quickly covered the train's floor. Then it all stopped suddenly. I looked up at the post-storm sky above and was greeted by a perfectly shaped rainbow. I joined the others in crying out for help.

"Help! Help me, please! My leg hurts!"

I slowly moved the rubble and debris that had fallen around me, but my leg was trapped. The blaring alarm kept going off. I looked around and saw a LED light flashing; it was some distance away, buried in the melting balls of storm-driven rain. Hoping it was a phone, I reached and reached, but the debris had my leg in a chokehold. No matter how hard I tried, I still couldn't move. At that moment, I gave in to the pain and lay there, listening to the loud alarm that continued to blare over the speakers. Without warning, a metal structure dangling from the gaping hole in the ceiling fell on me and woke me from this terrible nightmare.

The LED light on my phone, my blaring alarm clock, and a charley horse in my leg had invaded my dream, screeching at me to wake up. I reached over to turn off my phone and exhaled, "Phew."

"Whoa! That was intense."

The dreadful dream had ended. I was safe inside my condo in Atlanta. I eased the muscle cramp by walking around my spacious bedroom in circles. My dreams had been lucid since I was a child. Sometimes, I would dream of things that were both terrifying and true. I hoped that a tornado wreaking havoc on the airport would never come into existence.

THE RAIN WAS POURING down outside, and the wind seemed more robust. Floridians had taken it the worst, and now it was Georgia's turn. "Thank God for a shelter," I said while gazing out the wall of windows that surrounded my condo. Downtown Atlanta appeared desolate and gloomy. I was blasting my nostalgic boom box I got on my 10th birthday.

Years ago, my mom put it on sale at her once-a-decade yard sale. Luckily, my dad saw it and stashed it away for me. He knew this thing was like a best friend of mine when I was growing up.

I was listening to a mix I had curated on cassette before a short moment of silence filled my space as the power went out. Suddenly, the electricity blared through the wires, competing with the silent moment.

I decided to let the silence win. I turned off Ella Fitzgerald's angelic voice singing, *"Dream a little dream of me..."* and refilled my glass of Château Gillet. I got it as a souvenir while shooting in Bordeaux to add to my collection, but it didn't make it to my cellar. The ferocity of the water cycle drew me back to the window as I marveled at the storm thirty-two floors up in the sky. I've always loved a good rainy day. Of course, that's if I'm safely ensconced in the comfort of my home. The wind and rain had been putting on a show for hours, with the hurricane pushing northwest. At that moment, I couldn't help but think of how nature has such glorious abilities and formidable beauty.

"I'm so sorry how humanity is destroying you, Mother Earth," muttering regretfully as if the Earth might respond, "It will be alright, my child."

How could we be so blind and not agree to do whatever it takes to stop emitting carbon into our atmosphere? My bare feet left the warm spot I had made while gazing out the window in awe at the tropical storm. I walked across the cool, dark wooden floor to the snow-white faux fur rug. I opened the drawer of the side table and took out a pen and a notepad. I jotted down a reminder to discuss with Lauren about setting up

THE DREAM LIFE

another scuba shoot in the Great Barrier Reef before it becomes a complete grave. We could run a campaign to raise awareness of the danger humanity is causing to the reefs. My grandfather always told me that you can choose to be part of the problem or part of the solution. My house phone rang just as I walked over to hang this umpteenth note on the smorgasbord. I decided to let the machine answer it.

"Gene Rae, I hope you got the commonsense God gave you not to be out..."

"Hello, Mama," I said, picking up the phone and cutting my mother's rant short.

"I hope you're not going out in that storm trying to take somebody's pictures today. Tell whoever your life is more important than some pictures." My mom was notorious for knowing the weather at any given time for any geographic location. I went straight for my go-to closing argument statement to prevent the conversation from ending before it began.

"Mama, I capture the importance of the present moment in each take—those memories that can never be relived. It's more than just a picture, but I wouldn't expect you to understand my passion for photography." Since I can remember, my mother and I have often debated. She never understood why I would abandon a law degree to pursue a career in business and photographic technology.

"Well, I'm just saying." I held the phone, waiting to hear what my mom was "just saying," but she paused. I quickly changed the subject, asking her about the weather in Charleston and how everything was going. She shared that my dad had been locked in his workshop, building a canoe for weeks. Mama complained that the racket he'd been making was starting to get on her last nerve.

"Now he spends all his time out there in his new workshop building this canoe. I don't know how much more knocking and bumping I can stand to hear. I hardly see him except for supper and Jeopardy." My father was a gentle giant who loved two things for sure: building and Jeopardy! He knew all the answers to the questions. He'd often tell me,

"Babygirl, always make sure your questions and answers are evolving." I didn't understand what that meant as a kid, but I somehow lived by this philosophy. My mom kept sharing the minuscule issues of the day and life with my dad. I once again admired the storm.

Light was fading as darkness took over the sky, with ongoing rain and strong winds. My mom could talk for hours, effortlessly switching topics. They had been living in Charleston for two years since my dad semi-retired as a contractor, working on what he called "small tasks" projects. My mom was eager to retire fully from her role as a top sales executive in Manhattan and move to the suburbs. Now, I believe she was beginning to get cabin fever.

"Mom!" I cringed, "A huge lightning bolt just fell from the sky!" I shouted into the phone.

"Well, silly child, get off the telephone before you get an electric shock or something!" Then I heard the dial tone. Good, that did it.

Then the phone rang immediately after I placed it back on the receiver.

"I love you more, Mama!" I said, assuming my mother called back to say, I LOVE YOU.

Whenever she had had enough of our debate, my mother would hang up the phone, but would always call back within five minutes or so to say I LOVE YOU. Those three words seemed to put us back on common ground—a lukewarm state versus being hot or cold toward each other. I've adopted the instant reply, *I love you more.*

Then I heard a familiar voice say, "Oh no, you just got off the phone with Mrs. Roman? Is it a good time? Or should I call back? I'll call back." I interrupted her.

"No, Jessie. It's cool. How've you been, chica? I hate that we couldn't link last week when I was in New York. The Vogue party wasn't the same without you."

"Oh please, I'm just about over all these boring fashion week parties with these broke wannabes," she answered.

"What! Say it isn't so, J!" I gasped.

"Yes, Rae, I'm over the whole party scene," my best friend expressed.

"So, what's the word, thunderbird?" I asked her.

"I'm in Atlanta and was calling to see if you would accompany me to this party tonight?" Jessie backed-tracked.

"Wait...Didn't you just say..."

"I know, I know, but this is for work," she interrupted.

"Girl, are you, or are you not, in the state of Georgia right now? The tropical storm?" I reminded her.

"I hear all that, but this is for work, and there's a real chance that I would need your assistance on the project. There's a lot of coins to be made with this project, too." She paused.

Jessie always knew the way to grab my attention. Financial advantages!

"Keep talking," I replied. Just as she started to spill the info, my cell started ringing. As I walked over to retrieve it from the charger, I immediately saw Moon and Stars on the screen. I stopped in my tracks.

"J, let me call you right back. I need to take this call," I said to her.

"G, I need to know soon. The party is from ten until two in downtown Atlanta, and I don't want to go alone in this storm. You know Atlanta better than..."

"Give me five, 'kay?" I quickly answered my cell before Will hung up. "Baby, I love you. I've missed you. When are you coming to Atlanta? It's been too long," I went on and on. "We are getting a pounding from this storm."

He forcibly cleared his throat.

"Hello to you, as well, my love. I was calling to tell you that I planned to fly into Atlanta today to surprise you, but the flights are grounded at Hartsfield. So, I'm going to stay in New York until Thursday to finish some projects, so this weekend your body can have my undivided attention."

"Will, I've already reserved our favorite room at the Four Seasons, so don't even think about any funny business, Mister," I warned him.

"I promise, baby. I wouldn't miss our anniversary for the world."

"Okay. Let me call J back to get the details for this party tonight," I said, already dreading getting out there.

"Rae, I know you're not letting Jessie coax you into going out into a storm!" His tone sounded like my mom's.

"This is a business opportunity," I quickly stated.

"Well, what's more important, money or your safety?" Will asked.

"Flowers that are afraid of a little rain will never grow!" I snapped back as though I was defending myself from my mother's disparaging tone.

"Here you go with Rae's ranting colloquialisms." I could feel him rolling his eyes through the phone.

"It's not ranting if it's true." I ended the call and hit Jessie's line.

"So, what's the deets for the party?" I asked without letting her say hello.

"The manager of this emerging Atlanta artist wants me to assist him in promoting..."

"Wait! You're doing PR now?" I said, but she kept going.

"So, I'll be writing an article about his background and focusing on boosting his fan platform to generate interest. I need you to use your expertise behind the lens, of course. Just shadow his everyday life as an artist and take photos while he's working. You know, stuff like that. You game?"

"How much?" I inquired.

"Now remember, he's up and coming, and so is his budget," she stated, not giving a definite answer.

"So, you want me to shadow photo and film some young'un, for however long, stamp Rae Roman's signature on it, for pennies on the dollar? I know you know me better than that."

"What about all your philanthropy interests and give-back projects you like to undertake?" She called me out.

"Now, you know I'm the first person to donate and raise awareness for charity, but this ain't that. This artist is trying to advance his career and pockets, and so am I! Plus, I need to see if I can work this little project into my already compacted schedule."

"Genie, aren't you trying to get your freelance thing going? Maybe this could be a good opportunity to get your name out there."

Oh, so she's my publicist now, too, I thought. My name is already out there, maybe not on the building, but definitely in the credits. What she was advising wasn't absurd, though.

"I see the weather is starting to break. How long are you going to be in the Peach State?"

"Until Wednesday," she said, sounding defeated.

"Okay. Let me feel out the vibe tonight after meeting the artist, and we'll see. Text me when the car is outside."

"Great! Thanks, G!" She hung up the phone quickly, avoiding any further discussion on the subject.

CHAPTER 2

A Dollar and a Dream

Two hours later, Jessie called to say she would arrive in thirty minutes. I quickly got up and took a cold shower to refresh myself and gain energy. After this peaceful, quiet time at home, I needed to wake up. The rain even brought a pleasant afternoon nap. Still, work seems to follow me even on my day off. I changed into my prince-purple velvet halter dress, added a leather choker, tied my curly hair into a messy bun, and applied some Linkin Park after-dark lipstick. I grabbed my black high-top Chucks from the Chuck Taylor section in my shoe closet, sat on my chaise to get my black pearl earrings from the side table, put them on, and headed to the car. The stormy weather finally brought autumn air. When I got into the black Tahoe limo, the cold leather seats awakened my senses, making my nipples stand at attention through the velvet.

"Happy you could join us!" Jessie snarled at me.

"Uh oh, looks like someone brought their retro braless teen spirit personality out to play tonight. Are you trying to bring the 80s back tonight, G? By the way, your high beams are on." She laughed, observing my attire from head to toe.

"Didn't you know? I vowed never to let 80s fashion die." We laughed.

In no time, we reached Center Stage. The crowd mostly consisted of college-age students, standing around and staring at their phones. We stood at the door just a moment before the waitstaff escorted us to the VIP area. Bottles of Ciroc, Champagne, Hennessy, and chasers were already on the table. I immediately made Jessie a Hennessy with a splash of Coke and poured myself a Hennessy neat. We caught up on life over the loud music since she moved back to New York from London.

"What time is he coming? It's almost twelve?" I asked.

"Girl, you know how these artists are?" Jessie said, going for drink number two.

"This is exactly why I can't stand working with wannabe superstars. They have no consideration for people's time." Jessie vented.

"So why are you doing it?" I questioned her.

"The short answer?" she replied. "The money is green."

"How green?" I asked.

"Chartreuse!" she said with a straight face. We both laughed.

"But really, how green?" I remained on the subject.

"A bag if I play my cards right, and hopefully with interest," she admitted.

"And trying to pay me in peanuts?" I said sternly. "How long are you signed on for?"

"Only six months because I still have commitments with THE SUN. I'm taking a sabbatical, remember? After that, all I will have left is a dollar and a dream."

Just then, the artist in question and his entourage of eleven crowded into our space. This short, greasy kid wearing Spike Lee-looking glasses with no lenses walked up and greeted Jessie. She stood up, looking eye to eye with the guy.

Behind him stood a tall, muscular guy, with a supercalifragilisticexpialidocious swagger that reminded me of a lead singer in a '90s boy band. We locked eyes before a proper introduction, but I assumed he was the so-called artist. He had that telegenic look, kind of like a mash-up of Jodeci's Devanté and Ginuwine, but way sexier if you could believe it. His green-hazel eyes and ripped physique had the groupies lining up.

Jessie turned to me and said,

"This is Rae Roman, professional photographer, and my…" I stood and interjected.

"I like to say life's moment capturer, but professional photographer is fine. Enchante." The lean athletic fellow walked around his manager and Jessie and came directly to me.

"You are Rae Roman? The photographer, Rae Roman?" His interest caught me off guard.

"Just today, I read your interview in last month's Essence on the plane. You have such a way with words. I imagined what you looked like, the shape of your mouth. And man, oh man, words are not enough." *Was he trying to flirt because he wasn't doing a bad job?* I thought to myself. "Well, now that you've met me, does my appearance match my words?" I asked.

The young charmer started, "Let me tell you this: your beauty matches your words perfectly."

"Beauty and brains, printed on the résumé," I said with a smile. His manager politely nudged Jessie toward the admiring artist.

"Pablo, this is Jessie . She will be heading some of our projects in the PR division."

"Nice to meet you, Pablo. I'm Jessie," she said, handing the artist her card. "I'm going to be coordinating with you all to discuss the upcoming projects and dates for appearances I'm setting up for you. I'll follow up with you and Tony by the end of this week to arrange scheduling. I'm excited and looking forward to our new ventures!" Jessie said, forcing a smile as she turned to me. "And as I mentioned, this is Rae Roman, a professional photographer. She will be capturing what she calls 'litfe'—moments in the light of the life of an everyday artist— and doing photoshoots for ads and promotions we'll be using. Plus, she'll be collaborating on concepts for the cinema graphics for your shows and videos." I found myself thinking, *"Oh, really, I am?"* as Jessie signed my name to jobs and obligations.

"We live in a world where we record, photograph, and post everything now, so having her on our team will professionally and significantly boost your brand deals," Jessie said, applying her degrees in journalism and mass communication. She finally decided to leave that difficult boss in London, who didn't provide her with the resources for growth, and forge her own path. I was super proud of her for taking a leap of faith and pursuing her passion.

"Wait, I'll be working with this beauty?" Her words stopped him in his tracks.

"Yes, that is possible if she agrees to join the team. Are there any questions?"

"Only one. What will it take to put Rae Roman on my team?" he asked Jessie.

"First and foremost, you can't recruit someone of my caliber as a team player if the contract isn't green enough." His soul-penetrating eyes stared directly into mine and said,

"Name your shade of green, and I'll take it from there."

How old is this sweet talker? I thought to myself. Just then, his manager came to whisk him away to network around the party. Jessie followed the guys, and I fixed another straight.

As I started to relax, the charmer returned, and to my surprise, he had with him a bottle of Champagne. He sat down beside me and passed me a flute.

"What are we celebrating?" I asked.

"You and I working together, of course."

Really? The reverse psychology approach? I eyed him with a straight face and said,

"What is your name again?" I honestly had forgotten.

"I'm sorry," he said, setting his flute and the champagne down, and gently grabbed my hand. "Allow me to introduce myself formally. I'm Pablo tha Picasso." He kissed my hand. At that moment, I wanted to award him an Oscar for best charmer in a loft party scene and dismiss him from my vibe. However, I couldn't deny it; his charisma was spicy and electric.

"Oh wow…Pablo tha Picasso. Did you come up with that stage name all by yourself?" I asked sarcastically while reaching for my hand sanitizer.

"No, actually, my mom gave it to me. My real name is Pablo Lopez. I figured I'd add the Picasso, you know, since I'm an artist and all." That still remains to be determined, I thought.

"Is Rae Roman your actual name?" he asked.

"Yes," I told a white lie.

"Listen," I continued. "I know you're all excited about us working together for some reason. I received a brief overview of this opportunity only a few hours ago. I need to follow up with Jessie and review the commitments I've already made before making the final decision." He nodded and said,

"Okay, it sounds like you're a lady about business. I can respect that. Well, enough business talk for tonight," he reached back for the champagne and filled our glasses,

"Here's to you, Rae Roman, never have I ever been so captivated by someone's beauty and brains before as I have you." My poker face never let anyone know what I was genuinely thinking, so I gave him a slight smirk and said, "Cheers to wealth and great mental health."

LC burst into my office, shouting at the top of her lungs. "Where are the layouts? Where are the proofs? Raeeeeee! I told you to make sure you covered everything! You said you had this covered!" She kept going, pacing and panicking. Her cigarette and fire-red hair made her look as if her head were on fire.

"Just forget about it! Your greatest opportunity and my entire professional existence are ruined because of you! RAE ROMAN!" Her face turned crimson, and the veins in her neck bulged.

"You're fired! You will never work in this town again!" she said, then stomped out of the room and slammed the door so hard that the glass labeled **Rae Roman, Executive Director,** shattered inside.

Suddenly, my eyes snapped open from the nightmare, only to be bombarded by the sun blazing through the French doors of my bedroom. It was so bright I immediately squeezed my eyes shut. I felt around my sheets with my hands, searching for my phone with my eyes still closed. I reached for my nightstand and found it. I glanced at the time. "Shit!" I realized what my dream was trying to tell me. It was giving me the same warning as the eight missed calls from Lauren. I was late.

I felt nauseous and lethargic as I hurried to get ready. Suddenly, I felt bile rising in my throat, and I quickly ran into the bathroom. I grabbed my cell to call LC and tell her I had a "stomach virus" and to reschedule the shoot for tomorrow. Of course, she wasn't hearing that and demanded I get it done today. There was no point in pleading my case for health needs with her. She once came to work even after her car had been totaled with her inside.

"Okay, I'll be in at five," I told her. At least that gives me some time to shake off this hangover. Did I go that hard last night? I've never been a lightweight, but I don't even remember drinking that much to feel this way. When did I get home? I need to call Jessie to find out what happened last night because I'm drawing a blank.

I phoned Jessie to ask her about the night before.

"Well, well, well…" she answered. I got a twinge in the bottom of my gut.

"Call you right back," I said, then dashed to the bathroom. It had been a while since I last had a hangover. Feeling the remnants of the previous night, I headed straight for my recovery kit: ginger tea with honey, a lime wedge, a squeeze of orange juice, saltine crackers, and three aspirin. This routine worked wonders on long nights of filming the fertilization of coral polyps at the Great Barrier Reef. After being on that small boat and underwater, I was terribly seasick. However, the sickness didn't overshadow the experience of a lifetime, and I wouldn't have missed it for anything.

I decided to get some rest and call Jessie back later. The string of "wells" she uttered clued me in as to why I felt the way I did.

CHAPTER 3

Walking on a Dream

I arrived at the drafty warehouse a quarter 'til five. I could see the look on LC's face.

"Really, Rae, really?"

"Long night, you're familiar with the biz." This was my regular reply to her because, of course, she could sympathize with how she and I would go all night just to get what we were never given, a handout.

After ending an inconsistent relationship with my former boss and boyfriend, who was called Boss, I decided to move to Atlanta to take my professional photography career more seriously. I thought I would go straight into traveling the world while shooting for National Geographic. It turns out no one was interested in a melting pot chick from Brooklyn whose portfolio highlighted the culture of vagrants living in New York City and whose goal was to bring more shelters and job opportunities to vagrants through a docuseries. I mean, I was turned down everywhere, from top to bottom. It turns out that making a living by only shooting photos and filming this subject is seen as magical, like making invisible money appear, especially living in expensive-ass New York.

So, I moved to Atlanta and took on dead-end jobs until, one day, while waiting tables at the Sundial, I met Lauren Calloway. She had photos spread all over her table. It was tough to put down all the desserts she was "test tasting," as she called it. So, I slid over a small side table and wheeled out a dessert cart to give her more space. She looked up for the first time and said,

"Oh my gosh, you're beautiful. Ever thought about modeling?" I answered,

"Thank you for the compliment, but I have more of a behind-the-lens passion than an out-front one. Would it be okay if I help you empty your mind and tap into what you are trying to gather from these photos? My shift ends at 7, which is in about ten minutes." She gave me a blank stare.

"I don't see why not. I could use a little brain emptying," she laughed, using air quotes. We sat and talked until the restaurant closed. I shared with her my passion for giving people a perspective on life through the artistry of photography. We sat there, sharing dessert and ideas, and getting to know each other until the restaurant closed. Our

   THE DREAM LIFE

relationship was cemented in that moment. I went to work for her photography and film company, but we were partners, not boss and employee. She never tried to contain my ideas and workflow. I realized years later that meeting her at the Sundial that night was destiny. And the rest is history, as they say.

We finished the shoot around 10. While waiting for an Uber, I called Jessie back.

"Well, well, well!" It felt like a flashback.

"Please, J, lay it on me, easy girl."

"Is that what you told Pablo Lopez last night?" she clowned.

"C'mon, be easy. I still feel like shit."

"Genie, all I know is you all were deep in conversation, repeatedly selecting different bottles of champagne and tasting them with Hennessy. I came over to ask if you were ready to leave, but I could see in your eyes that you were caught up in one of your sessions. I kept talking business with his manager, Tony; the next thing I knew, you had left with him!" I put my hand over my mouth as I gasped.

"Say it ain't so, J!"

"Now wait, now. I have no idea what you two were conversing about, nor what happened after you all left, but..." she paused.

"But! But what?" I couldn't handle the suspense.

"I did see him kiss you," she revealed.

"No way! Deadass?" I knew she had to be joking, or I hoped she'd say psych. However, she did not.

"Deadass!" she concurred.

I found it hard to believe that I was making out with a stranger, especially a potential client. My number one rule was never to mix business and pleasure. It was a lesson I had to learn the hard way.

When I arrived back at my condo, I immediately began taking off each article of clothing, creating a trail to the shower.

"Alexa, play anything from Empire of the Sun," I said, as I stripped off layer after layer. I hit the steam button and started my meditation. I still had a queasy feeling in my gut. Was it the hangover or the unknown truths about what happened the night before?

I was still half asleep when I woke up to the smell of sizzling bacon and a migraine. A nostalgic smile spread across my face as if I were waking up after spending the night at Nana's. She always prepared a grand breakfast buffet when she babysat on Saturday mornings, especially when Mom had deadlines to meet. Then I realized that unless my mom had forced the useless concierge to give her access to my condo again, there was a stranger in my home, and I needed to be cautious. I went to the closet to retrieve Betty Sue and slowly crept toward my kitchen. The closer I got, the more pungent the smell of burning bacon became. I released the safety on my gun and held it upright in the intruder's path.

"Pablo! What the hell are you doing in my house? Get the hell out of my house! I'm calling 9-1-1 right now!" I grabbed my house phone from the stand and started to dial the number.

"Okay, first don't shoot me, and second, calm down." He said with surprising calmness, his hands raised slightly toward the ceiling. He then started walking toward me. I took a step closer to him, clinching Betty Sue tightly.

    THE DREAM LIFE

"Don't take another step closer. You're trespassing, and I will shoot you where you stand if you don't leave now!" He then dropped to his knees and raised his hands.

"Rae, I am asking you to calm down and listen."

"Don't ask me to calm down. You're a stranger, and you're in my house making breakfast! Why? How the fuck did you get in my house!" I yelled.

"I'm just following up on my part of the deal to get you on my team," he exclaimed.

"Part of the deal?" I questioned.

"You gave me a list of things I have to do before you agree to work with Jessie on helping me get my name on the big screen."

"I would never give a stranger permission to come to my residence. Are you crazy?!" I confessed, but I was starting to think about what had happened last night. Did I make some drunken agreement with this guy?

"Are you feeling OKAY, Rae?" he asked, as if he thought I was losing it.

"I sure am, but you're not about to be. Get the hell out, stranger!" I kept yelling.

"Remember, you gave this stranger a key last night," he said, pulling out a familiar set of keys from his pocket with a unicorn key chain. The smell of the burning bacon made my head pound more. As I lowered the gun, he released a deep exhale. I walked out on the terrace to get some air. The morning dew had fallen, and the air was crisp and cool.

"What the hell happened last night?" I asked myself. I was waiting for a reply that never came because, at that instant, I woke up frantically from the dream. I looked at my phone, and it was only 3 a.m. I got up to make a late-night trip to the kitchen. When I opened the Sub-Zero fridge, I stood there, letting the cold air refresh me. I took out an icepack from the freezer and propped it on my head to relieve the still-present migraine. Ever since I could remember, my dreams have always been lucid and sometimes aligned with my real life. They led to many restless nights, awakenings, and intuitive ideas.

I couldn't go back to sleep, so I decided to get some work done instead. Two years ago, I set a goal to deepen my passion for photography by building a darkroom in the vacant unit below. It was smaller than my penthouse but large enough to serve as a suite for my parents when they visited. Fortunately, I knew a stellar contractor who could do the job right and happened to own the building. The best dad ever. He never understood my eclectic ideas, but he always supported them. I turned off the light, played Outkast's Aquemini album, and got to work.

***

Thursday.
Will is expected to arrive today, and I eagerly await seeing him. We've been on-and-off lovers since high school, but now that we've matured and found our individual paths, our relationship has deepened in respect and understanding. Neither of us expected him to enter the corporate world, but that's where his degree took him. When he visited Atlanta, we'd go out for drinks. The night usually ended in one of our beds.

     THE DREAM LIFE

We were like fire and ice at times, but for nearly two years, we've been committed. He's been commuting between Atlanta and New York for eight months, yet it hasn't affected us, as I also frequently traveling between Atlanta and the world. One time, he appeared unexpectedly at a job I was doing in Paris—a night shoot beneath the Champs-Élysées arch. While adjusting my lens for a high-society wedding shoot, I noticed a man in the distance in my shot who kept posing awkwardly.

I walked over to ask him to chill out. As I got closer, I recognized this stature and a blushing smile that looked all too familiar. Just then, he pulled out a bouquet of long-stemmed white orchids from behind his back; it stopped me in my tracks. I flashed a big, cognizant grin and ran to him, leaping into his arms.

"Can I take you out for a Parisian dinner in the City of Lights, my love?" he asked, trying and failing to pretend that he didn't already know the answer.

"I'm so happy it's you. I thought a Frenchman was about to catch these hands." We laughed. "So, will you have some time for dinner and dance with me underneath this beautiful starry night?" he continued to wonder.

"Are you kidding me? You flew across the pond, interrupted my shoot, and you expect me to call it an early night?" I paused. "You got it, dude!" He laughed, and we shared a long embrace. That night was magical.

It was almost nine in the morning. I called to find out when Will's flight would arrive, but his assistant said he was still in a meeting. Jessie texted me a picture of a yes, no, or maybe GIF with checkboxes. I had to get down to the bottom line of what this new adventure would entail.

"Hey, girl. Listen, we need to set up a meeting to go over all the details with that artist guy..." I blurted out as soon as she mumbled hello.

"Oh, so now he's that artist guy?" she shaded me.

"J, you know I never mix business and pleasure, so I'm sure whatever happened when I left with the guy was harmless. We probably just shared an Uber." I said, hoping that was the truth.

"But getting back to the subject, when do you think we could meet?" I was forcing myself to stay on point.

"We can meet today if you want?" she asked.

"Sounds good," I agreed. "We can meet at this little consignment boutique in the Highlands in about an hour. I need to get a dress for tonight."

"What's going on tonight?" she inquired.

"Will is coming back to town for our anniversary this weekend, so if we could do the meeting soon, around noon, that would be great," I shared.

"Okay, send me the location."

"Gotcha, I'm doing it now," I said, searching maps for the pin to send to her.

After a quick shower, I chose comfort. I wore a worn T-shirt featuring Biggie with a crown, oversized jogger pants, and a jean jacket. I swung open the French doors to my shoe closet. "Who wants to dance?" I asked as if my shoes could reply. I reached for my Buttas without hesitation.

I went downstairs to my studio to pick up the pictures I had developed to drop them off at the agency. Just then, a thought occurred to me: I needed to get a quick wax before tonight's escapades.

The Body Wax Studio was my go-to place for waxing every part of my body. Vanessa used gentle waxing techniques and always squeezed me in with little to no wait. After catching up with Vanessa, I headed to the agency to drop off the photos. As soon as I walked into my office, LC popped her head in, pulling on a Virginia Slim. She knew I hated it when she smoked in my office.

"Did you get those pictures printed?" I nodded yes. "Okay, will you bind them?" She was on one of her tailspins today, I could tell. When I didn't immediately answer her, she snapped.

"Can't you hear? Is that a yes or no, Rae?" I snapped back at her.

"First of all, put the cigarette out or get out. Second, Jon Jon has already taken them to the layout department. Lastly, why are you already spazzing this early in the morning?" She plopped down on the couch in my office like it was a therapist's couch.

"Rae, I got into a fight with my ex's bitch last night."

"Whaaat?!" I dragged the word out.

"So lately, Tate and I have been trying to get that old thang back. We went out to dinner last night, and everything was going great, so I decided to sleep with him." I looked up from my computer at her.

"Wow, you must have been desperate," I responded.

"Rae, everybody doesn't have fellas on roll call like you!" She sat up and barked at me.

"LC, I've been in a committed relationship with Will for two years, remember? Not counting the on-and-off puppy love years. So, I don't think that qualifies me as having fellas on roll call." I said, trying to convince her otherwise.

"But you could. A whole list. If I were your age and body, you just don't know!" She reclined back on the couch, pulling out her handy-dandy signature fan, and began fanning herself profusely. I stopped typing and turned to her. "Was that a compliment? You rarely give compliments. Are you feeling okay, girl?" I asked her, now genuinely concerned.

"See, I'm screwed all up today."

LC was always the straightforward, poised professional, independent in every sense, a goddess not to be toyed with. She had been with Tate, who seemed to be made by God just for her, going on twenty-three years, until she caught him in bed with some twenty-two-year-old. She said, "I just let it slide because I knew how much of a bitch I was to him over the years. People make mistakes sometimes, Rae. One hasn't lived until you've had to bite the bullet and forgive the person who hurt you the most, when all you really want to do is walk away."

"LC, you said it yourself. Tate had completely changed from the man who made you fall head over heels in love. Someone who knows you and loves you with truth doesn't waver on that love. You are a beautiful person inside and out. You may be a little nuts to deal with sometimes, but that doesn't give Tate the right to dip his dick elsewhere," I said stridently, now trying to boost her confidence.

"You're too young to understand yet. Life changes you, Rae. Maybe for the good, the bad, or something in between,

   THE DREAM LIFE

but as you grow, you learn that things that seem detrimental and trivial aren't. And every problem doesn't warrant a definitive end."

Suddenly, my phone's vibration started to quake my glass desk. "I need to take this, LC." She immediately left my office, closing the door behind her.

"Good morning, my honey," I answered.

"Yo, honey bunny! Bad news, the team and I have a…."

"So, you're canceling on us?" I interrupted.

"Rae, if you could just let me speak, you'll know that I'm not canceling our anniversary," he paused. "But I do need to reschedule for next weekend." I held the phone, feeling the impulse to tell him that he could go to hell for canceling a long-awaited weekend. It seemed like we'd scheduled plans for the last few months, only to have him keep pushing them off.

"Hello, are you still there, Rae?"

"I'm here," I said, letting out a disappointed sigh. "Will, you knew how much we needed to reconnect this weekend."

"Of course, I know, and the Four Seasons will still be there next weekend. We must get this deal done before Monday, Rae. Other factors have come into play, sidetracking the merger. So, I'm dealing with two monsters here. Please, don't be a third. You know I'll make it up to you, and I plan to, the long way, if you know what I mean."

"Oh, yeah? The long way, huh? Oh, how I have missed thee."

"So, are we good, my love?" he asked.

"I guess," I replied dryly, feeling disappointed. *Damn,* I thought, all that bikini wax pain for nothing.

After my call with Will, I felt emotionally compromised. To clear my mind, I grabbed my Leica and took a stroll. The cool weather awakened my senses and made me notice aesthetics everywhere. I eventually reached Underground Atlanta, an area with a mix of gentrification and poverty, reminding me of NYC neighborhoods. As I crossed Broad Street, I noticed a woman rummaging through trash, collecting aluminum cans into a nearly full bag. She was small and looked to be dressed in all her layers against the cold air. I paused in the street and quietly took photos of her, omitting her face. Over the years, through my dedicated photography to support the homeless, I've aimed to avoid making vagrants feel mocked, especially since many struggle with depression and mental health issues. I then crossed the street and approached her.

"Good morning, I'm Rae. How are you doing today?" The lady ignored me and continued to rummage through the garbage, pulling out cans.

"Are you hungry? Do you need any help with money or shelter? There's a mission not too far from here," she looked up at me.

"Yep, I need some help," she instructed me.

"Hold this bag." I put my camera around my neck and did as she told me. The trash smell was awful, but it didn't seem to bother her one bit.

"What's your name, if you don't mind me asking?" She looked at me as if she had seen me for the first time.

"Mary Francis," she answered.

"Oh, really, my grandmother's name is Mary, too." She stopped what she was doing and gave me a hopeful look.

"Are you my grand-baby?" Her eyes had a rosy stare.

"No, ma'am, but it's nice to meet you, Ms. Mary Francis."

"I'd sure wish my son would let me meet my grand-baby. What's your name, baby?"

"I'm Rae Roman."

"Well, thank you, young lady, for your help." She took the bag, tied it, and threw it on her cart.

"Ms. Mary Francis, are you hungry? I can take you somewhere to get food or here…." I reached into my pockets to scrounge up what little money I had on me and passed it to her.

"The good Lord gave me the will to survive and make a living for myself. You keep your money, sugar. I can eat for weeks off my can money." I watched as she walked to the next trash can. She pulled out a new bag and continued collecting cans. I was honestly baffled. People often assume vagrants are lazy members of society and want free handouts, but Ms. Mary Francis has shown me something today. She has the will to survive and is not conforming to societal norms to do so. She had brightened up my day, and she didn't even know it.

CHAPTER 4

"I'll be dreaming of you."

It was almost noon. I needed to call Jessie to nix our link-up at the consignment store since Will had to reschedule. But when I went for my phone, I couldn't find it. I guess I left it at the office. LC was standing in the doorway of the elevator when I got back, smoking a freshly lit cigarette, and holding my cell.

"Girl, what did I tell you about leaving your phone behind and making yourself unreachable?"

"That it shows characteristics of being unreliable," I responded dryly and shrugged.

"Right!" she beamed.

"But did anybody die?" I asked facetiously.

"What am I going to do with you?"

"Sorry to inform you, but there is little that can be done. Many have tried, none have succeeded."

"Jessie's been blowing you up. What is she up to these days?"

"She wants me to join her on this new work venture."

"What is it?" LC asked.

"Working up-and-coming music artist, but you know how I feel about working with people in that industry."

"Yes, but as long as the retainer is in your favor, there shouldn't be a problem, right?"

"True. The artist did say name my color green."

"Well, what's the problem, my dear?" LC asked, as if money were a cure-all.

"We shall see," I told her. The tricks usually outweigh the treats when working with the music industry.

Just as I walked into the darkroom to develop the photos I had taken of Ms. Mary Francis, my phone started ringing. It was Jessie again. I quickly sent her a text.

CANCEL THE MEETING. CALL YOU SOON.

I turned on the Bruno Mars playlist on the workstation iPod and got to work.

Before I knew it, the day had flown by. It was a quarter after five. I started packing my work into my briefcase to take home for my three-day weekend—which should have been a staycation at the Four Seasons—when LC barged into my office.

"I need you for a shoot tomorrow at the Fox Theatre. Are you available?"

"I know I told you my plans fell through, but I'm still taking off tomorrow, LC." I stared at her with a straight face.

"Sheesh, Rae, put away the death stare. That's why I asked if you are available, rather than demanding it. Besides, what else are you going to do but mope and drink Chardonnay because Will bailed?" I gave her the *if looks could kill* eye again.

"Don't give me that look, Rae. You're the best I've got. Just say yes, please!" I remained quiet. "What are you going to do? Eat donuts and sleep all day on a Friday? C'mon…"

"You're right… I'll do pizza instead of donuts!" I joked.

"C'mon, Rae… I'll pay you triple time," she crossed her fingers, pleading as if she didn't have other staff who could've done the job.

"Fine. What time?"

"You are the best! Around noon, cool?"

"Okay, have a good night." I walked out with her still standing in my office and headed for the elevator. Jonathan came rushing up to me.

"Hey, Rae! Wait up!"

"Yes, Jon Jon?"

"Wanna come out with us tonight to this loft party not far from your place? You are off tomorrow, so I don't want to hear that "I'll be too tired at work tomorrow" line you've been giving me lately."

"You are about to hear that exact line because I'll be working tomorrow after all, plus truth be told, I don't want to,"

   THE DREAM LIFE

I said, staring at the ascending elevator light as I waited for it to arrive at my floor. I was in no mood to party.

"Well, if you change your mind, here's the flyer." I glanced at the offprint and saw it would be hosted by Pablo tha Picasso.

"Hey Jon Jon," I called him back. "Who invited you to this party?"

"One of my friends from Clark who does promotions." The elevator opened. I walked in, observing the info on the flyer.

"Will we see you there?" I kept looking at the flyer as the door closed on Jonathan and his unanswered question.

On the way home, I phoned Jessie. She sent me an automatic reply:

"Call you back in five." As I walked into my building, I saw the concierge who had a thing for me, so I pretended to be on my phone to avoid small talk.

"Hey, Rae! You got a second?" he yelled out. *How rude. Doesn't he see I'm on the phone?* I thought. I pointed to my phone like, 'Can't you see I'm on the phone, dumbass?' I kept walking. He followed me to the elevator and handed me a lovely flower arrangement.

"These are for you, beautiful," he said, handing them over like a swaddled baby. "They're not from me. If I sent you flowers, I would have had them bedazzled with diamonds because you're truly a diamond, Rae. Rare, beautiful, and invaluable." I took the flowers and stepped onto the elevator.

"Thank you, Raymond." My phone rang as I was holding it to my ear.

"Hey, J. I'm on the elevator, so my phone may disconnect."

"Okay, I'll be brief," she answered.

"What's the sketch?" The call dropped. I hit her line once I made it into my condo.

"Genie, I'm asking you again. Are you going to sign the six-month contract to work with Pablo?" That daunting dream I had of him burning bacon flashed into my thoughts.

"I apologize, Jessie. I know I've been unreachable today. The answer to your question is yes."

"Yes? Deadass?" She sounded surprised and enthusiastic.

"Yes, J, I want to support you on your new business venture."

"Fanfuckingtastic! I love you, girl! Thank you, Genie! We're having a listening party tonight. Are you available to come to sign the contract?"

"Oh yeah, at a loft, right? My coworker already invited me."

"Really? How did your coworker find out about it?"

"He said one of his college buddies invited him."

"Well, great. Pablo is getting some traction."

"What time are you heading there?" I asked her.

"Around nine. Do you want to go together?"

"Sure, but I can't stay too late. I have to work tomorrow."

"I thought you had a three-day weekend?" she asked.

"Me too. Will has a merger that's giving him hell, so LC asked me to do a shoot tomorrow."

"He canceled on you, G?"

"He said he needed to reschedule for next weekend due to work. I was so pissed, J. We haven't connected in months. If you know what I mean."

"Really, G?"

"Really, J, but don't get me started on that. I'm about to refresh myself from this day with some Chardonnay. Call me when you are about 30 minutes out."

"Okay, girl. Yes, whoosah and relax. I'll let you know when I'm in route.

I poured myself a nice full glass and put on some chillax Lofi Hip Hop. The Sonos surround sound eased me into a peaceful place. Before I knew it, I was sound asleep on the couch. Jessie's 'on the way' text woke me up a little after nine p.m. I jumped in the shower to refresh myself. The cold water hitting my skin felt like tiny snowflakes, causing me to get goosebumps. I stepped out of the bath onto the wooden bamboo shower mat and reached for my terry-cloth robe to warm my frigid body. I entered my closet and sat on my chaise. What did I feel like tonight, thrill or chill? I'm sure the crowd would be young, so I opted for a laid-back vibe. I quickly threw on my gray DRESSED TO KILL tour KISS t-shirt and some dark, ripped, fitted jeans.

I finished the look with oversized accessories, my long suede camel-colored coat, and biker boots. My phone started ringing. I guessed it was Jessie, but it turned out to be Will. I ignored the call. He followed the missed call with a text.

SO, DID YOU GET THE FLOWERS?

The message read. I was so busy dodging Raymond's ass and contacting Jessie that I forgot to read the note attached to the flowers. I walked into my foyer, retrieved the card from the dancing orchids, and read the message.

HAPPY ANNIVERSARY, MY LOVE. I'M DEEPLY SORRY FOR SPOILING OUR ANNIVERSARY WEEKEND RENDEZVOUS AT THE FOUR SEASONS. I WILL MAKE THIS UP TO YOU! TWO YEARS OF STRONG COMMITMENT, NINETY-EIGHT MORE TO GO.

Commitment? What a damn contradiction, I thought. I wanted to stay mad at him, but I knew it was just sexual frustration. We'd both had our share of cancellations for work matters. I brushed the tension aside, not allowing it to ruin my vibe tonight. On the way to the lobby, I texted him back.

YES, THEY ARE BEAUTIFUL, THANK YOU!

Jessie was waiting right in front of the door. Raymond ran over and opened the lobby door for me. "You be safe tonight, Rae. I'll be here when you get back. I'm working a double tonight."

"Good night, Raymond." The words rushed from my mouth.

We walked into the steep-ceiling loft and headed straight to the cash bar.

"What are you drinking tonight, J?"

"Think I'll have a Cosmo tonight," she said, tapping her finger against her chin while studying the drink selection as if she were at a full bar.

　　　　　THE DREAM LIFE

"We'll have a Cosmo with plenty of cherries and a Tennessee Honey neat," she said to the bartender.

I turned around to scope the crowd. It was an upbeat vibe in the air. A couple of college girls were dancing to a song with an Atlanta snap feel in the middle of the floor. Maybe something from a local artist. Jessie started to bob her head after a few sips, which meant that the bartender had made her cocktail to perfection.

"Let's scope the crowd," she said, starting to walk away. Just then, the lights went off. We instantly caught each other's hands. A sultry voice came over the speaker that I recognized as Pablo's.

"Welcome to the turn-up, ladies and gentlemen." The small crowd softly cheered. Laser lights started flashing, and the music came back on in sync with the light show.

Jessie and I stood there trying to figure out what was coming next.

"This is Pablo's new song," she said.

"Go figure," I replied.

"Let's try to find his manager so you can sign the contract." She weaved her arm around mine and led the way.

"FYI, I'll get the contract back to his team after I give it a good look over, but I'm not signing anything at some dimly lit party. Mama ain't raise no fool."

"Figured you would want your attorney man to look over it, anyway. What are you doing this weekend, since y'all's plans went up in smoke?" What was his lame ass excuse for canceling, by the way?

"Rescheduling," I interjected. She raised her sharp eyebrow at me.

"Genie, you know you need to check his ass. How's he gonna cancel, I mean reschedule, y'all's anniversary for a damn job that can be here today and gone tomorrow?"

"I could be here today and gone tomorrow also, J." She hugged me and said,

"Don't say that." I changed the subject.

"Why haven't any record labels signed him yet? His sound is original, and his lyrics make sense. Then again, conscious music is not relatable to today's demeaning and vain society."

"You just answered your own question, G." I turned around and saw Pablo standing at the far end of the party, talking to a group of girls. They were all dressed like they were DTF anyone who says they are in the industry. In other words, groupies.

"There's our client J," I said, still looking at him and admiring his pack of groupies. We walked around the people who were starting to gather in the middle of the loft, turning it into a dance floor. Jessie greeted Pablo, interrupting the lascivious gaze he was giving the groupies.

"Hi, Pablo. Rae is here to discuss the terms of the contract. Is there a private room we can go into?" Suddenly, everyone within earshot focused their gaze on me. The group of females standing there sized up Jessie and me as if to say, 'how dare she come to snatch the meat we were about to feast on?' Pablo had an adoring look in his eye. I walked over to them and said,

"Don't worry, girls. I won't keep him too long," Pablo retorted.

  THE DREAM LIFE

"You can keep me as long as you please." They dispersed after that statement, their departure accompanied by huffs and puffs. Pablo walked us back to a tiny office tucked away from the party, where we couldn't even hear the music.

"Ladies," he said as he pulled out the office chairs from the desk for Jessie and me.

"Enjoying the party so far?" I bobbed my head.

"It's a vibe," Jessie nodded. He went over to a mid-sized fridge and pulled out some chilled champagne flutes.

"Is this where you live?" I asked.

"Nah, it's rented."

"Where is home for you?" I asked.

"Technically, LA, but my home is in my head." I gave him a captivating look.

"I have a question for you, Pablo," I said, looking directly at him.

"I need to know exactly what else you are expecting from me that doesn't appear written in the contract." He hesitated slightly and asked, "What do you mean?"

"It just seems your intentions are leading …" I stopped myself and looked at Jessie. She immediately understood that I wanted to speak with him alone. I waited until she was out of the room and the door had closed. I walked around to his desk, sat at his side, and made eye-to-eye contact with him.

"Please allow me to be honest and straightforward, Pablo. When I sign that contract, you are my client. There is no in-between, in the gray, or misconceptions. I work with you. Not for you." Pablo kept pouring the bubbly as if his mind was elsewhere.

"Are you hearing me?" I asked.

"I'm listening to every word. Go on, say whatever you need to get off your chest." I continued.

"Just remember, stick to the contract, and we'll work together just fine, but no more flirting and trying to charm my panties off. Also, I'll have Jessie arrange an official meeting with your team to discuss the contract and such. We can meet at my office."

He leaned back in the office chair and rubbed his palms together. "All that sounds good, but if I'm also allowed to be honest, having a beauty like you around will make it hard not to want to indulge in business and pleasure." He clenched two flutes and stood up.

"Trust me. No one has ever successfully done both without it getting messy." He took a step closer, passed me the champagne, and said, "Well, to successfully making this money." We clinked our glasses together, eyed each other once again, and shared a sensual exchange. A knock at the door broke our glare. Jessie re-entered the room.

"Everything good in here?"

"Yes, partner." I passed her a glass, and we cheered on our new partnerships. We went back out to join the party and continued celebrating our new business deal. The crowd had grown hype while we were in the back. There was a great atmosphere. The DJ was mixing all the old jams with the new. Jessie and I migrated to the makeshift dance floor and started to do old-school dances. Pablo joined us. He was slaying all the retro dances when the DJ started mixing Run DMC.

"Yo, this DJ is fresh," I complimented.

"Hell yeah! He's my homie from high school. He knows I like old-school music." Just then, he out Jodeci's Feenin'. I looked over at Jessie. She was already starting to slow-whine on some fellow she was doing the Running Man with a few slaps back. Suddenly, I remembered I had to work tomorrow, and it was later than I had planned to stay out.

"I'm about to catch an Uber," I whispered in her ear.

"Text me when you get home," she responded. I gave her a nod and turned back to Pablo.

"I have to get going." He gently clutched my wrist.

"One last dance." He pulled me onto him like we were about to do the Waltz.

"Nah, it's late, and I have a shoot tomorrow," I resisted. He smelled so damn good I could have melted in his grasp.

"Remember, we just agreed, business only," I said to him, but honestly, I was trying to remind myself.

"A deal of a lifetime. You are a beautiful human, and I am attached to your essence," he continued. "Your scent, your rich caramel skin, I would bite you if it wasn't a crime." I stopped dancing.

"I have to go."

"Okay. Do you need me to arrange a car for you?"

"No, I'm about to send for one. You can walk me out, though?"

"My lady." He put his arm up as though he were accompanying me to a debutante's ball. We stayed quiet in the elevator. When we got into the lobby, I sat in the lounge area, and he sat with me.

"I wanted to ask you something."

"What is it, Rae?"

"What happened when we left the party last night?"

"That was a fun night," he stated. "We took a trip to the nearby lake in my vintage car. We stared at the stars while unloading our guts to each other. Then the most remarkable thing happened. You let me kiss your soft lips. I gushed all day to the homies about it..." He paused and then began to laugh so hard. He stopped when he could tell I wasn't joking.

"Be serious," I said, folding my arms.

"What happened is the same thing that's happening now. I walked you out, and you left in an Uber. Past that, I don't know. Why did you ask?"

"I had a very foggy memory and a wild dream. Jessie said we spent all night talking and we left together, which concerned me because I normally would never leave with someone I had just met."

"Wait, did you dream of me?" He laughed, then noticed the look on my face and cleared his throat. "You were pretty wasted. I could tell. I've had many of those nights. I offered to ride home with you to make sure you got home safely, but you adamantly refused." I gave him a bashful look.

"But it's all good, Rae. Nothing crazy happened if that's what you were wondering."

"My Uber is almost here." I stood up from the lounge area and walked out of the tall glass doors. Pablo followed right behind me as I left the building. There was a moment of awkward silence as we stood for a few more minutes waiting for the Uber. When the car pulled up, he opened the door and whispered in my ear, "I'll be dreaming of you. Until next time, Rae Roman."

   THE DREAM LIFE

Friday morning, I was stuck in a false awakening. I continued the unsuccessful process of trying to wake up again and again until finally, my eyes popped open. There was a chill in the air. I crawled under the covers to the end of the bed and grabbed my terry cloth robe off the ottoman to warm my naked body. LC had called me three times and left messages, so I messaged her back.

ON THE WAY.

I headed to the shower and turned on the steam to clear my head for the day ahead. While singing Badu's *On and On*, I started thinking about Will and where we were going as a couple. The constant cancellations weren't healthy for our relationship. I could admit that.

We were just two peas in a pod that clicked perfectly. Even in junior high, I could see myself being his lover for life. Of course, we had gone from playing all those games during our young and dumb days to now becoming financially stable and somewhat decent human beings. But after all that, marriage never seemed to come up as often as one might expect. Now that we were at the top of our game, the game was all we could see. Despite everything, I couldn't help asking myself, *Is there more?*

When I came out of the shower, I decided to FaceTime him for some unannounced cybersex. He ignored my FaceTime request and texted me back.

HELLO, SWEET LIPS. WALKING INTO A MEETING, SO I DON'T HAVE TIME TO GET A HARD-ON SEEING YOUR BEAUTIFUL FACE.

I responded,
BABE, I NEEDED SOME MORNING CYBERSEX TO GET MY DAY OFF TO A GREAT START. I JUST GOT OUT OF THE STEAMY SHOWER, AND MY BODY IS DRIPPING WET ALL OVER.

He replied,
WISH I COULD BE THERE IN PERSON TO SUCK THE WETNESS OFF YOUR SUPPLE NIPPLES, BUT THE MEETING HAS STARTED. HIT ME TONIGHT.

"Fuck," I grunted. I pulled out my vibrator from the bedside table for a DIY quickie. I rubbed my soft nipples until they were erect from thinking of Will feeding me his long-way pleaser down my throat. I finished myself off and then rested there, feeling partially satisfied. I didn't want to get up after that, but there was money to be made. I headed to my closet and threw on my black cropped turtleneck, some ashy black jeans, and my black Gucci belt, paired with my black Tom Ford booties. I was indeed looking ready for a Black Panther's position. I took my red plaid cowgirl flannel shirt, wrapped it around my waist, and then went into the kitchen to fix myself a quick smoothie. I booked an Uber and put on my Chucks. I glanced at the flower bouquet sitting like a centerpiece on the marble table in my foyer. Then I got an idea. I could fly into New York after work and surprise Will.

    THE DREAM LIFE

"Hey, LC." She shot me an evil eye because I arrived an hour late. The early meeting with Pablo's team ran over. LC knew she had to respect that this was originally my day off and that I was doing her a favor. "What are you doing here?" I asked her. Even though LC didn't have to, she sometimes showed up and actively participated in the jobs her company took on. She once told me retirement would make her go senile, so she'd rather keep working.

"Yeah, well, the cast director and I go way back. Had to see if he was still something worth giving a second look at in our seasoned age. Tate's not the only one that has some mojo left."

"I heard that!" We shared a laugh and a high-five.

"We're going to do an empty shoot of the stage set up, makeup and hair, dress rehearsal, and the play, then the entire cast on stage following the show. They are doing some behind-the-scenes documentary." She directed me on our to-do list for the day, and I nodded at her and said,

"Okay, let's get busy." The play was truly fantastic. It was a love story—an elegy to A MIDSUMMER NIGHT'S DREAM/ROMEO AND JULIET—about two young adults falling in love, but a crazy/beautiful love that ended their young lives. After we wrapped for the day, LC came over to me and handed me two tickets to a Broadway play.

"What are these?" I questioned.

"Comp tickets the director gave me, and I'm giving them to you. Catch the red-eye and surprise Will with a little downtime at the theatre."

"I was honestly considering surprising him myself. Should I, though? He's been working hard on this deal. His urgent need to reschedule might not welcome a surprise visit." She delivered her famous 'just do it' speech by telling me with one word,

"Go!" She walked off, leaving me standing with the tickets in one hand and the camera in the other. I reached into my pocket for my phone to search for flights leaving tonight. Nothing was available until five am tomorrow.

When I got home, I noticed I had two missed calls from Jessie. I called her back. "Are you free to shoot a roll tonight? Tony wanted to get some nightlife photos of the Atlanta skyline from the Jackson State Bridge. He also wants some graffiti backgrounds if you know a place."

"Krog Street Tunnel. Maybe Little Five Points."

"Cool, so you're game?"

"Uh…Tonight though? It's been a long day at the theatre. Plus, I'm trying to catch the red eye to New York."

"Even better, Pablo is flying into New York late tonight."

"Okay, and?" I know she wasn't suggesting what I thought.

"Maybe you can catch a ride on the plane with him after the shoot. I'm sure he wouldn't mind."

"Don't even try reverse psychology, J. It isn't going to work tonight. I'm too exhausted. Also, what happened to Pablo's financial budget? I thought he was an up-and-coming music artist with a struggling budget. I wouldn't expect him to be able to afford chartering a plane."

  THE DREAM LIFE

"The flight is just a favor. You know how it works. You scratch someone's back, and they scratch yours in return. Ah! Come on, Genie! We have deadlines and schedules to meet."

"What does any of that have to do with you calling me at the last minute and expecting me to jump? I haven't received any information for work scheduling and dates..."

She interrupted. "Rae, sometimes freelancers have to go off schedules and scripts. Plus, you signed the contract, so all lights are green, okay?" I stayed quiet. My silence always meant victory for her, and she knew it. Then she said,

"Silence…yes, thanks, girl! Sending you a car around 6:30. Remember, we want sunset views, so bring whatever camera of yours that will make the shots look incandescent."

I met Pablo and the crew at a quarter 'til seven. We took some stunning shots of the tangerine, violet-hued sunset sky. We drove to the Krog Street Tunnel and then to Little Five Points for graffiti shots and street photography of the local dwellers. As I was packing up my equipment, I saw Pablo in the view, slowly making his way closer and closer to me. Suddenly, I looked up, and there he was.

"Can I help you with anything?" I looked up at his silhouette statue gracing me.

"No, I got it. Thanks."

"It's not a problem. I don't mind."

"No, it's not that. I just have a certain technique for packing my equipment away."

"Oh, okay, so you're OCD." I cut him with a look.

"Excuse me!" He walked over and passed my tripod to me.

"Please don't get offended. As you said in the interview, I understand you like perfecting the little things to make your craft exponentially abundant."

"And which interview was this?"

"The one where you were conducting your boss's interview in some magazine. I think it was Elle."

"You certainly keep up with my magazine appearances, huh? And predominantly women's magazines, too, I see. Are you attracted to me or…"

"What are you trying to say?"

"Are you into men?" I bluntly asked.

"Hell no! If I haven't made myself clear to you by now, let me know. First and foremost, I love women. Always have, always will. Also, I'm into you, Ms. Rae Roman! However, I agreed to our contractual agreement, not to mix business and pleasure, so it is what it is, and I respect that. But damn, Ma, it's true I had a lil' crush on you before we ever met." He was talking in circles. I must admit Pablo had that whip appeal. Music started to blast from a nearby speaker.

"Yo, this is my new single that's out now. How does it sound?"

My ears were instantly attracted to the song's beat, and the lyrics weren't bad either. I bobbed my head and said,

"Sounds good." Then I asked,

"Will I still be able to catch a ride on your private jet to New York tonight?"

"You can take a ride on whatever you like, Rae." I rolled my eyes.

"What time are we leaving and from where?"

"Around 10. I can get my driver to pick you up on our way to the airport if you want. You live downtown, too, right?"

"Yeah, I do. Okay, I'll text you my address. Thank you."

CHAPTER 5

Dream Lover

It was almost ten when Pablo texted me; he was just minutes away. I texted him back; I'll be at the entrance. Will and I were bound for a love affair one way or another. I grabbed my Louie packed with a weekend full of pleasure.

When I got into the Tahoe limo, there was only Pablo, which surprised me because he's usually with an entourage.

"Where's your entourage?" was the first thing I asked.

"They're meeting us there." Our airport ride was mainly small talk as we stayed occupied with our gadgets. When we arrived, the airport was deserted.

"Where's your team?" I inquired.

"My manager texted me that something came up, and they would have to catch a domestic flight in the morning. So, it's just us." For some reason, my stomach started to feel queasy.

Anytime I had to fly, I would always get anxious. It's improved a lot, but you're sure to feel it on a plane when you're afraid of heights, especially on smaller jets. As we got out of the limo, he asked, "What are your plans in New York, if you don't mind me asking?" I gave him a 'mind your business' look.

"Don't tell me you're spending your entire weekend working?" Pablo said as if he wasn't doing the same thing.

"Aren't you working this weekend as well?" I asked with an annoyed tone.

"Yeah, but I'm an artist. There's always some pleasure that comes with my line of work," he answered, coming close behind me and helping me put my Louie in the stowaway closet. I turned around, now face-to-face with him. He smelled yummy and clean.

"In my line of work, there's always business interfering with pleasure," I said, creating more space between us.

"Well, we have to change that. Come to my show tonight," he said eagerly.

"I'm surprising my boyfriend for our anniversary this weekend."

"Why didn't I know you had a boyfriend?" He sounded offended.

"Maybe 'cause you never asked," I replied. I've never been someone who openly offers information about my private life.

"Well, let me ask you this. Why is he not surprising you?"

"Because he's closing a deal in New York," I said with an attitude, wanting to reply, Who are you to be questioning me about my relationship?

"Don't get so defensive. I just know if I were him…." He paused, giving me eye-to-eye contact with those steamy hazel-green eyes. "Whatever would wait 'til whenever for you."

"Easier said than done when you're not operating billion-dollar business deals."

"Well, excuse the poverty outta me," he said, seeming slightly offended.

We ascended to over 30,000 feet in the troposphere; the flight felt smooth and relaxing. I called the flight attendant to bring me another vodka to calm my nerves for the night ahead with Will. Pablo came over and sat across from me. He didn't say anything; he just looked at me.

"What are you thinking about with your cute self?" he asked me.

"Just trying to stay chill. Not a big fan of heights. What are your plans in the Big Apple?" I asked him, trying to distract myself from my fear of flying.

"Well, I have this show to do tonight at SOBs and some press tomorrow—business as usual. What are your plans with your boyfriend?" he asked sarcastically.

"I'm surprising him with tickets to a show on Broadway and dinner at his favorite restaurant." Pablo giggled to himself.

"I knew you were one of those prim and proper women," he said, laughing. Pablo and I got to know each other for what felt like hours. He seemed to be a decent person based on the stories he shared. His father unexpectedly died one year after his family moved to Atlanta from California. He was only

 THE DREAM LIFE

fourteen, making him the man of the house for his mother and younger brother. He worked at the AJC and Six Flags just to demonstrate responsibility and how to be a provider for his little brother, even though his father had left them financially comfortable. As usual, I shared basic details about myself because of my contractual duties, never anything as personal as my dad being my adoptive father, or that my biological dad was killed by a drunk driver when I was six months old. I began to drift off to sleep. I woke up from what felt like a long nap.

"Pablo, how much longer? Feels like we've been flying forever." He replied,

"With you… a century, I hope. Rae, listen, I'm going to take you to Italy tonight. I've got a villa on the Amalfi Coast, and we'll come back on Monday. Unless you would like to stay longer?" I was stuck. My tongue was under submission.

"Say what now?" It was all my brain could manage to utter.

"If you're not cool with it, we could reschedule for another weekend. This offer is good until November."

"What offer?" I asked him.

"An offer I got to stay at this 5-star villa in Italy. It's kind of like that timeshare shit, but on a much larger scale. I'm not considering buying, but a free trip is a free trip, and I couldn't think of anyone else more befitting to accompany me than you. You earned it. You've been working nonstop, and you don't deserve to be canceled on by your man. You deserve to be surprised with a luxury trip to a luxury villa, and Rae, what's more luxurious than the Amalfi Coast, I ask you?"

Many thoughts started to cross my mind. Then I almost threw myself into a panic, but I remained calm and took out our contract. I stood up and handed it to him.

"Pablo, let me remind you that we are under contract. You will be required to pay the full amount specified in our agreement if you breach any of its clauses. Not in installments, but in full immediately, and I walk. More than anything, I never granted permission to be whisked away by you. You don't even really know if you like that."

"Let's change that," he said as he stood up, grabbed me by the waist, and pulled me in.

"Rae, fuck that contract. I never dreamed in a million years that I would ever be in your presence in this lifetime. Now that I am, I will do whatever it takes to make you mine. Allow this to happen, please." He kissed me long and deep. He swept me off my feet and laid me on the bed in the jet. He unrelentingly kissed me, then he began unzipping my hoodie. I wanted to pull away, but our connection was so explosive we could have created a star. He pulled off my black leggings and kissed me from my neck down to my royal blue laced thong. He didn't bother taking them off; he kissed lower and lower. My love zones began to throb. He slowly crept his hands up my back, now sucking on my nipples through the matching royal blue laced bra, making the fabric as wet as my southbound region. He popped my bra latch, unleashing my breast into his warm mouth. "Pablo, we can't do this. Pablo, stop!" He stopped and looked at me. We are here."

"Already!" I exclaimed.

"How long did I sleep?" Again, he said, "We are here," nudging my shoulder. I started putting my clothes back on, feeling disoriented about what the hell was going on. Pablo nudged my shoulder again. My eyes snapped open, and my instincts kicked in. I swatted his hand away from my shoulder. "What? Where?" I had fallen asleep, stretched out in the chair where I had sat when we took off.

"Whoa, it's okay, Rae, didn't mean to startle you. We are here in New York, remember?"

"I'm sorry. How long have we been here?"

"We landed about ten minutes ago. I didn't want to wake you. You were sleeping so peacefully. I have to get ready for tonight, so we are about to dip. I have a car dropping me off at my cousin's house in Brooklyn."

"Oh, really, I grew up in Brooklyn. Where does your cousin live?"

"Over on Ocean Avenue. Anyway," he went on, "I can get him to drop you off wherever. Manhattan, perhaps?" he probed.

"Actually, yes, but I've arranged for a car to pick me up."

"Well, you have my number. When are you flying back?" he asked as we de-boarded the plane.

After that erotic slumber, I felt the need to keep it short with him. I could still feel the moistness from the dream.

"I'm not sure." I took my luggage away from him and said,

"Thanks for the ride." I caught myself as soon as the words left my mouth.

"Anytime," he said with a smirk. The driver put my bags in the trunk of my limo and opened the door.

"Until we meet again, Rae Roman."

The ride from Queens to Manhattan took almost an hour that late Friday night. When I arrived at The Plaza hotel, I wanted to surprise Will with my presence, so I called him from the lobby and told him I was catching a flight to New York first thing in the morning. I also informed him to call the front desk to give me access. I figured he was still at the office. He tried to convince me to stay in Atlanta, and he wouldn't have time to go to the theatre because the deal wouldn't be closed until Monday. I asked him if he had left the office yet, and he said yes, calling it a night. I told him I was still coming, and if it was just to have lunch with him, that would be perfect. I could tell he was in bed because he started to sleep-talk.

"What's your room number again?" I asked him.

"Eleven-eleven," he said while releasing a loud yawn. I hung up the phone and walked over to the bar. I ordered a martini and replied to some emails before going up to Will's room. The old white guy sitting on the other side of the bar kept eyeing me. I ignored him and continued sending and replying to emails. I looked up, and he was sitting next to me, staring.

"Can I help you?" I asked him.

"Hello, pretty lady, I'm Oliver." He extended his hand for me to shake. Of course, I wasn't about to touch his hand. Instead, I responded.

"Oliver… Is that with or without the twist?"

The old man laughed and asked, "Can I refill your martini, pretty lady?"

"I'm about to call it a night, but thank you anyway."

"Well, would you like to accompany me up to my hotel room for a nightcap?"

"Excuse me!" I was appalled. What did he think I was, some hooker working the bars?

"Mr. Oliver, sir, you have the wrong one. I'm not a woman of the night."

"No problem, you can be the woman for this night. Trust me. I can make it worth your while. You are just the way I like my women to be. With your smooth, beautiful, cinnamon-brown skin. Nothing like my pale ex-wife." When he threw his black card on the bar, I knew it was time for me to exit stage left. I stood up. I tossed the rest of my drink back and repeated myself.

"As I said, you have the wrong woman." I grabbed some cash out of my bag to pay the tab and walked away before I had to go off on this demented old colorist freak. As I walked out of the bar, that encounter with Oliver sparked an idea in my head. I went into the lobby bathroom to freshen up. I disrobed and misted my skin with some Ferragamo. I used my fingers to wet-comb my hair, giving it a pool-dipped appearance. I put my trench coat back on, only buttoning my intimate areas. I located my "So Kate" black patent leather red bottoms, along with matching sexy elbow-length gloves, that I had packed in my Louie for playtime. I pulled out a tube of Mac Rouge Matte lipstick. Will and I would often role-play whenever we met up in different cities while traveling for work. The old creep at the bar would have been me in that script, and Will would have been the unlawful high-priced escort, game to do whatever to get me off.

When I arrived at room eleven-ten, I pretended to be housekeeping, knocking at the door, saying HOUSEKEEPING in a disguised voice, but Will kept saying No, thank you. As I continued to bang, the door suddenly flung open, and there stood my handsome honey. All dreamy-eyed.

"Rae," he said, rubbing his eyes.

"Who's Rae? I'm Cinnamon, and I'm your private escort for tonight."

"Rae, didn't I just get off the phone with you?" I refused to let him break my role-play.

"Aht-aht call me Cinnamon," I said.

"Well, Cinnamon, is it? I have an important deadline to meet, so I need some rest because…." I covered his mouth with the shiny black gloves and stayed in character.

"Ms. Rae Roman has already paid for the night, sir, so I suggest you relax and let Cinnamon handle the rest." Will was visibly too tired to continue putting up a fight, so he caved. He led the way into his bedroom; I pushed him down on the bed. I gradually open my trench coat, first revealing my royal blue laced bra with my nipples already erect. I turned my back to him and continued unbuttoning and teasing him until I undid the trench coat. I turned to look back at him, lying there with his long way bulging through his briefs. I began to drape the Burberry intentionally, feeling the soft plaid lining against my skin, teasing him by not revealing all of me at once. I turned around, dropped my coat swiftly, and then climbed around his lovely shaft, easing his briefs down around his knees. Then I began kissing, nibbling, and licking him. I flicked my tongue around the rim of his tip, then began to take him deeper into another dimension with my mouth. He flipped me over and proceeded to penetrate my love spot. The sensation was

    THE DREAM LIFE

unbelievably exotic. His strokes were fulfilling a long-awaited scratch that desired more than a dildo. I couldn't retain myself any longer. I came furiously hard and fast, then began to collapse. Will continued stroking and said,

"Oh, hell no. I know you didn't fly all the way to New York to get knocked out in the first round. We're not done yet. Can you drive a stick, Cinnamon?" I lay there feeling all the feels. Then a rush of insatiability came over my G-spot. I positioned myself on top of his erect shaft, riding like a cowgirl, but Will wouldn't allow Cinnamon to steal the show. He stood up at once with our pleasure zones still attached and gently laid me back on the bed, slowly grinding his hips. This guy wouldn't let up.

"You missed this good loving, didn't you?" he said nothing, just gave me a wink. We sang songs of passion cries for a few more rounds, then he collapsed inside of me. We shared some light pillow talk, and then we refreshed and rebooted. At this point, I was only wearing my thigh-high boots and long gloves. Will was butt-ass naked, with Big Willy swinging from left to right.

"Damn girl, I worked up an appetite. Let's order room service." I walked over to the couch and sat down. I crossed my legs, then slowly and widely uncrossed them.

"Bon appétit," I said, resembling Sharon Stone. He smiled. Will walked over and headed south to surrender his tongue between my legs. He flipped my body into a plow pose. His tongue entered my wetness and delivered shockwaves through my body. He stood over my elevated, pulsating vagina and did a low squat, placing his shaft deep into me, thrusting back and forth.

"William! Aye, bien Papi!" He took Big Wil out and began to slap the tip of his dick on my clit, then went back to licking me so seductively. He scooped me off the couch and threw me on the bed, and said,

"Let's take a walk on the wild side, Cinnamon." Making love to Will always took my love zones on a trip, and we seemed to travel around the world that night. He had always been a dream lover in-between the sheets. Walking into the bathroom on my tippy toes, I felt that familiar vibrating sensation in my love zone. I sat down on the porcelain toilet, and my urination began to squirt out sporadically. I could feel the remnants of the orgasms. I sighed in exhaustion as I took off my boots and gloves. I went to the sink, grabbed a rag from the hook, opened a new soap pack, and continued with a refreshing bath. As I cleaned myself, I could feel my sweet spot reminisce, reminded by the warm rag. I went to the minibar, grabbed a Perrier bottle, and hydrated myself. I looked over at Will, who was lying there paralyzed, staring at me. He softly said, "Come here." I went over and climbed on top of him. We rested there, flesh to flesh. He kissed me on my forehead.

"Happy anniversary, my love. Thank you for surprising me. I needed this." Then we drifted off to Dreamland.

     THE DREAM LIFE

CHAPTER 6

TEEN DREAM

When I awoke that next morning, I felt completely re-energized. While doing some light bed stretches, I noticed a note on the bedside table that read,

You rocked my world,
You know you did…
Let's meet for lunch around noon.

I looked at the radio clock; it was already a quarter 'til twelve. The time prompted me to leap out of bed as if I were late for work. I searched the room for my phone to call Will and couldn't find it anywhere, so I reached for the hotel's phone instead.

"Hello, honey bunny. Why have you not been answering your phone?"

"My apologies. I have no idea where my cell phone is. I'm just waking up. I haven't slept this late in I don't remember when." He laughed.

"Just admit it. This dick had you on Cloud Ten last night. It's hard to come down from a high like that," he said, continuing to laugh.

"I will admit Cloud Ten is a place I'd like to visit more often because it has been pretty dull down here on the surface level."

"Nights like last night are best in moderation. That way you won't get too sprung," he said boastfully.

"Too late!" I replied, erupting in laughter.

"Are you able to meet me for a slice?" he asked.

"A slice with you? Always. Where were you thinking?"

"That little spot you used to like to go to in high school, remember?"

"Vinnie's?!" I gasped in shock.

"Yeah, Vinnie's."

"I haven't eaten at Vinnie's in years."

"I know, me either."

"But that's in Brooklyn. Do you have time? It's almost twelve now, and I haven't started moving yet, babe. You think they are still open?"

He dismissed my doubts and said, "Yes, and yes. I googled it. It's still there."

"They are! Wow, I guess the economic woes didn't come for them. That's good to hear."

Will and I met up at the subway station. Then, we got on the L train and headed to Vinnie's for a slice in the afternoon. I got my favorite, which was still on the menu, a Vinnie's Great Grandma Pizza. A sense of nostalgia came over me as we strolled into Vinnie's. I felt as though I was sixteen and falling head over heels with my first love again.

I rose on the tips of my toes, wrapped my arms around Will's neck, and peered into his eyes. "I love being back here with you. Thank you for taking time away from your busy schedule to have a slice with me."

He looked back at me with admiration. We used to come here after school activities. I had been a gymnast and cheerleader since I could walk, and Will was the star athlete in every sport. We were the cliché high school lovebirds. Our bond was unbreakable from the start because we were both motivated to succeed beyond what was expected from young Black kids growing up in Brooklyn in the '80s. Vinnie's brought us back together after a rough split years earlier. This was the place where we shared many slices and secrets back in the day. The good old days, but we didn't realize that then. One day, he paged me after curfew to meet him ASAP. When I entered and saw him sitting in our booth, I knew something was off from his face. Will was a true Cancer man. He struggled to express his feelings directly. After sitting quietly for nearly two hours, I finally got the truth from him. He said, "I don't wanna go home. Let's have a second slice." By the time the pizza was out of the oven, he had tears quietly flowing down his face.

"Will, please just tell me what's wrong. Did something happen? You know you can tell me anything," I pleaded with him. He didn't say a word. Finally, when it was almost curfew, he told me that his brother had been killed by a stray bullet while playing streetball. That was the worst memory we had at Vinnie's. It was here he broke the news that he didn't want to go to NYU, as we had planned since ninth grade; he wanted to go to Morehouse instead. Also, the place where I cried my eyes out to him when my mom threatened to write me off because I planned to quit law school and switch my major to business with a minor in photographic technology. One of the most life-changing revelations came the night we graduated from high school. We decided to go there with some friends to fuel up before the shenanigans began. I pulled Will outside, away from our friends.

"Yo, ma, we 'bout to have a wild night tonight. You ready?" Will asked, hugging and kissing me on the neck.

"Will, I'm pregnant." He stopped kissing and stared at me, speechless. This grand reveal quickly derailed his plans for a wild night out. The timing couldn't have been better. He was about to leave for Atlanta, and I was set to attend Howard in the fall. Yes, indeed. Vinnie's has held many memories.

We had a cozy afternoon catching up on everything happening in our lives, both together and apart. I told Will about my new business venture with rising artist Pablo Picasso. He mentioned he was feeling burnt out at work and wanted us to go to Fiji for Christmas instead of staying in the cabins with

THE DREAM LIFE

his family, which had been a complete disaster the previous year.

"So, what's after lunch at Vinnie's?"

"Well, actually, I also have to meet up with one of my colleagues for a quick meeting on this side of town. He lives not too far from this area. His babysitter called in sick, so he couldn't come to the city."

"So, this so-called impromptu day in Brooklyn worked out perfectly for you," I said, teasing him. "No worries. Will. I don't mind. Handle your business, babe."

"Ah, baby, you're so understanding. By the way, I'm going to call a car to take you back to the city or wherever you need to go, but first, we're going to do a little exploring." I looked at him in amazement.

"Well, aren't you full of surprises today!" I exclaimed. It felt so good to be back home with him. We had come so far from battling over what love meant to us as individuals. Combining the two ideas had been even trickier. It's funny how, as much as you want to give love to someone, you can't if they have never experienced what genuine self-love is first. However, it's also peculiar how every soul has an innate ability to long for love even before experiences ever occur. How Will and I are still walking around Brooklyn today is a mystery to me. It was destiny, I suppose.

We arrived at the Brooklyn Botanic Garden, and it was stunning.

"Oh wow, this is beautiful. What gave you this idea?" I asked suspiciously.

"One of my colleagues told me about this rolling street art exhibit they have, knowing how much you love street art. I noticed it's close to Vinnie's, which inspired me to spend the day in Brooklyn. It's been a while since I had some quality time with my shorty in the great BK, na mean," he paused. "You know, there are a lot of redevelopments happening in this area. Do you ever think about moving back?"

"To Brooklyn? Hell no. It's too expensive," I said.

"That's everywhere worth living in today's market. I'd love for us to come back here and start a family. I want our children to grow up like we did, running around these tough streets. It'll make them strong too, just like us. Nah ma, we ain't having no little wimpy kids," he muttered as if he were trying to sell me on his dreams. I looked around at the changing scenery of the concrete jungles we would tread through to catch the bus home after a slice at Vinnie's, which now looked unfamiliar to me. "Yep, gentrification is evident all over Brooklyn," was all I added to his dreams about moving back.

Will and I spent over an hour walking around the different exhibits and reconnecting. His phone began to ring, and he slowed up a bit; I kept walking, admiring the African bird of paradise plant.

"Hey, my queen." Will snuck up behind me with a hug and a kiss on the neck. "I have to get back to work. By the way, I've arranged a massage at the hotel's spa for you. You can add a facial or whatever you want; just charge it to the room. If you want, we can go out for a late dinner. Just don't kill me if I'm running too late." I smiled and kissed him on the cheek.

"No pressure, my love. I will definitely take you up on that massage." I arrived back at the hotel later that afternoon.

     THE DREAM LIFE

While my phone was on airplane mode, I received 9-1-1 alerts from Lauren. I dialed her immediately. She answered, "Hey girl, there's a Cosmo cover shoot tomorrow in Greenwich Village. Will you be able to do it?"

Now the truth comes to light on why you encouraged me to come to NY this weekend. It was all a ploy, huh, LC? Do you think I came to New York City on my anniversary just to be called away for work? Right now, I'm pulling up to my hotel, about to get a massage. So, honey. Bye!

Sometimes, I had to remind LC that not everyone chooses to live their lives behind the lens 24/7 like she does. Over the years of working with her, I realized I was doing more work than truly living. I made a promise to myself when I was younger: to enjoy my years more and not get caught up in the 9 to 5 grind, which in my demanding world is more like 24/7. Yet, work and money always seemed to take priority over that promise. But not today. It had been a perfect afternoon, and nothing could kill my vibe.

When I arrived at the spa and checked in, the staff member offered me some cucumber detox water and escorted me to the massage room. I undressed and put on the terry cloth robe. The smell of lavender drifting through the air and the soothing water fountain began to relax me. I sat down on the chaise, sipping my water. There was a knock at the door. "Come in."

A tall, muscular man walked in. He was a bowl of milk chocolate muscles and quite attractive.

"Good afternoon and welcome. I'm Kuntar. I'll be your masseuse today. Do you have any problem areas you would like me to work out?" I grabbed my right shoulder and told him about the injury I'd sustained during my athletic years, which aches at times.

"No worries, I will take care of all of that for you." I settled myself on the small, warm bed, and Kuntar got to work. This guy had the magic touch. He majestically pulled, pushed, and popped out all my kinks. He even stretched me and popped my neck. I felt like silly putty in Kuntar's grasp. He was putting me to bed. Right when I started drifting off to Dreamland, my phone started blaring, disrupting the peaceful vibe in the cozy little room.

"I'm so sorry. I thought it was on silent. Excuse me for a moment," I said, getting off the warm bed to quiet my phone, not waiting for an answer. It was Jessie. I texted her back, *call you in an hour.* Instantly, I felt chill bumps on my breasts. I forgot I was topless. I covered my breasts and looked back at the masseuse.

"I'm sorry for the interruption," I said, giving him a shy smirk.

"No apologies needed, Ms. Roman. Shall we continue?" he smiled. Kuntar finished giving me the massage of a lifetime. He even went over thirty minutes. When I put his tip in the envelope, a note was inside reading, 'You have a beautiful body. Let's do this again sometime,' with his number attached. I slipped his tip inside and left the note. Then I reminded myself that this was one of the best massages I'd ever had, so I took out my cell and created a contact named KUNTAR (ANOINTED HANDS), just in case I felt the need for them again.

CHAPTER 7

Our Heroes' Dream

After my massage, I went back to the room to take a nice hot bath. What a wonderful day it has been. I remembered I hadn't yet told Will about the tickets to tonight's show.

"Oh well. He's busy anyway," I said to myself. Then I thought of Boss. He loves any excuse to get all Dapper Dan, and it had been far too long since we rallied. I shot him a text, instantly regretting my choice. I grabbed two mini bottles of red wine from the fridge and drew a steamy bath. While I was undressing, my cell began to ring. It was Jessie again. I rushed out a "Hey girl. What's up?"

"Oooo, you sound busy. You're getting your groove back, aren't you, G?" We both erupted in laughter.

"Hell yeah! Now, what do you want so I can get back to grooving?"

She took a deep sigh. "Well, it's Pablo-related, but I can save it for when you get back in the A. Hopefully, it will be all figured out by then." I've known her long enough to know when something was up.

"What's the matter, J?"

"Pablo was arrested," she shared.

"What! For what?!" I screamed, shocked.

"I have no clue yet. It happened in the wee hours of the morning near the club where he was supposed to perform. I was trying to get in touch with you to see if everything went okay with the flight and how everything was last night."

"Everything went fine. He went his way, I went mine. Is he okay? Have you talked with him or someone in his group? I hope he's okay," I said with concern in my voice.

"Damn girl, you jonesing for Pablo or something?" she asked, laughing.

"Girl, please. I have a man, okay… A wonderful, successful, handsome man."

"Whatever, Genie! I've noticed that Pablo is infatuated with your scent, and don't play dumb and tell me you haven't noticed it, too." I couldn't deny; my best friend had nailed it.

"Of course. I've noticed this, which is why I'm unable to work for him. J, I'm not about to compromise my name for some twenty-something-year-old kid singer slash rapper slash thug life wannabe that perpetuates the life cycle of the stereotype that black men must experience the same systemic

    THE DREAM LIFE

struggles. And go figure, now he's in jail. This is not what the Black Panthers fought for. This was not their dream."

"Damn, Angela Davis. Calm down." She sounded offended by my words.

"Well, I'm just telling it how it is in real life, it's a trap, Jessie, and you know it!"

"Let me talk with Pablo about his flirtatious ways. I am sure we can resolve this without getting hasty, Gene Rae Roman." She used my full name to show she was serious.

At that moment, I caught my reflection. "Then again, who could blame the fellow? Being around all this beauty is bound to put a spell on any straight man, hell, maybe gay men too," I stood there admiring my curvaceous, melanin-dripped figure in the mirror.

"See, you know you're a bad bitch too, so get off the boy's little nuts and give him a break, G." We shared a laugh.

"Listen, I have to go. I'll call you when I'm back in town." I hung up, not giving her time to respond.

As I hung the comfy bathrobe I was wearing on the door hook, my cell started ringing again, and I immediately answered without looking and said, "Jessie, can you please let me enjoy my weekend?" thinking she was calling back to ask me not to end the contract with Pablo.

"Jessie? As in Jessie Grey? You all still kicking it, huh?" It was Boss. I froze for a moment, forgetting I even texted him. I thought the invitation for him to accompany me to Broadway would be a long shot in the dark, and after that massage, I just felt like room service and relaxing, not going anywhere.

A drawn-out 'heeeyyy' is all I could congregate.

Gene Roman

"So, The Gene Rae Roman wants to link up tonight? With me? I can't believe! Where you taking me, baller shot caller? Wait! Where's what's his face? Or have ya kicked that phony-baloney to the curb?"

"Again, hey, Boss. How are you? "

"I'm doing well, Ma. Can't complain… I can't believe I'm even talking to you right now…I called you last week. Figured you and that Mark was out, shopping at Costco or doing some domestic shit. You gotta start hitin' me back, Shorty. We could be getting hella bread together in Atlanta. I have a lot of moving parts down there. Let me know when you're ready to jump on the money train. But for real, for real, Boogie, it's been a hot minute, though. How you been, Ma? Did that square ever man up and marry you?"

"Boss, you should know me well enough to know marriage will never be the ultimate goal of happiness for me."

"Oh, really? Is that why you turned down the eight-karat pear-shaped rock I proposed to you with eight years ago? I know you desire more than some two-bit Wall Street prep boy. I know you. You like prim and proper but love a roughneck…." I turned off the running water and sat on the bathtub ledge, instantly regretting texting this bull-headed ex of mine, who was somehow still a loyal friend and a business partner. Apparently, he was still harboring ill feelings toward how I had turned down his proposal. I interrupted his rant.

"I have to go, Boss. I'll call you later?" Click went the end button, and I put my phone on airplane mode. Boss was as precise as his name implied. This man owned clubs in Harlem, D.C., and Vegas, and also had stakes in numerous profitable ventures. 'No' was not a term Boss had often heard before we

 THE DREAM LIFE

met. Before the LC and I era, I was an undergrad law student, cartwheeling through life, when I decided to start exploring photography, which became a passionate hobby for combating the stress of law school. We met when I was twenty, working as an assistant shooter and equipment manager to a small-time photographer named Johan; he had hired him for a magazine layout at his club in Vegas. He flew us out there on a private jet—my first time on a chartered plane. I knew then that I wanted to live this life of luxury and glamour rather than be stuck in a courtroom all day.

On the first day of the shoot, Boss had a seafood feast catered for the crew during lunch, but Johan suffered a severe allergic reaction to the food and nearly died. Luckily, the paramedics were able to revive and stabilize him. Boss was unaware of what was happening because he had left just before the feast arrived. His assistant told me he would be flying to the East Coast to handle some business and likely find someone else to finish the project. Since I was told he would cancel the rest of the shoot, deal with Johan, and find another qualified photographer, I decided to go out and enjoy my last night in Vegas with some of the dancers I'd met. Later that night, while walking down Las Vegas Boulevard back to The Cosmopolitan to pack for my early flight home, I received a call from an unknown number. The caller—the New Yorker— asked, "Yo, this is Boss…How would you like to make a shit load of money by finishing up the Vegas shoot for a brother?" He was very straightforward. I thought it was a good chance to get my foot in the door, so I said 'yes' without wholly considering what the job entailed, but I trusted my skills and knew my methods could stand on their own. The next day, when I arrived at the club, I felt nervous because I knew this shoot could launch my success. My unique ability to capture perfect moments at the right angles and make them stand out to viewers was rare and had yet to be seen. But this was my shot to put my name on a project that could be featured professionally. I rearranged some of what the first shooter had done the previous day and turned it into cinematic theater. Boss walked in while I was working. He yelled, "Cut! Nobody told you to put my girls in full costume and change everything around! Change it back! Girls, tops off, now!"

"No," I said as he continued to rant. "First of all, excuse me, Mr. Boss sir, trust me, I got this. This concept will get more traction than nudes, which will be heavily censored or denied."

"Dead that! I booked you all to do the job I asked for, so do it. Okay?"

"No." The words fell off my lips without hesitation, even though I was nervous as hell. A silence fell upon the room.

"You know what, little girl? No one tells me no!"

"Well, I just did."

"Oh, so you, Boogie-Down-Bronx bad, huh?

For some reason, he just gave me a smirk and walked away. He sat in one of the cozy velvet VIP booths, lit a cigar, and said, "Well, get to work, Lil Ms. Boogie-Down. Chop! Chop! Time is money!" He clapped. "Let's see what you got."

The rest was history. Aside from his insolence, Boss was a great mentor and a better friend than a boyfriend. He taught me many things about the entertainment industry and life in general. I admired his determination and hustle. I was still living in D.C. when I met him. He would fly me to different

     THE DREAM LIFE

cities for both business and pleasure. The funny thing, too, is that Will and I happened to reunite at one of Boss's clubs in NYC. It had been five years since our messy breakup, and at that moment, fate seemed to bring us back together. He looked good in his crisp, casual V-neck tee and well-fitting dark denim jeans. I was standing on the ledge of the upstairs VIP area when I noticed his familiar stance in the crowd.

The ripped warrior-like creature turned around, and I all but fainted.

"Will!" I yelled his name as if he could hear my voice through the loud music and crowd. He did. He looked right in my direction but couldn't tell where the voice was coming from. Boss questioned me, "Who is Will?" My mind went blank.

I said, "My first love. I'll be right back." Many questions started running through my mind as I made my way down to see him. What should I say? I wondered if he was here with a girl. Is he still mad at me? When I finally reached him, he was gone. I looked around, but he was nowhere to be found. I walked to the bar to get a drink. I stood there feeling like someone had pulled the rug out from under me, stabbing the orange peel into my Basil Hayden with the straw.

"Gene Rae Roman." When I heard him say my name, it was like someone had stopped my heart. I slowly turned around. He stared at me quietly. I stared back.

"William Dean Jones." Just as we were acting like we didn't know each other for most of our lives, he embraced me. As I allowed him to cradle me, I inhaled that memorable manly cologne smell of his. He let go but was still holding onto me.

"Did you call my name?"

"Me? No, I'm just sipping my drink."

It sounded like I heard a distant but nearby *Will* hit my eardrum. For some reason, when I heard it, I thought of you." I snickered.

"It was you? Wasn't it?" I nodded and laughed. The chemistry between us was still undeniable. Will and I started dating again, but nonexclusively, a year later. I ended my love affair with Boss after he tried to atone for his scandalous ways by proposing to me with a flashy pear-shaped diamond. I mean, chicken head after chicken head would confront and try to fight me over him. I decided to let the streets have him. I knew I didn't truly love Boss the way someone should love a spouse. His controlling nature didn't want anyone else to have me, but he enjoyed the women who constantly threw themselves at him without fault. They all wanted the celebrity lifestyle he offered. It didn't end with official break-up verbiage like *it's over* or *we're done*. One day, I just had enough.

I bought a one-way ticket to Atlanta and never looked back. He called days after my absence, not asking for forgiveness, but just to say, "You deserve the best, Boogie. I'm forever in your debt, and I will always have your back, no matter who or what comes and goes." My retainer fee stayed active, and business kept going as usual. Boss has that quality—*through hell and high water, I'll be there*— *action above all* mentality that I respect more than anything. It had been years since we hung out outside of work, so I decided to let him be my Broadway escort tonight. But I didn't feel the need to explain why we didn't work out, not for the hundredth time. Boss is also why I have a strict business-only clause in my contracts. Working in this lifestyle has brought me face-to-face with many suitors who swore they'd do anything to have me on their pleasure payroll.

I submerged my body in the steaming lavender-scented oatmeal water. As I sat there soaking up the aromatherapy, I thought about how I was letting the situation with Pablo affect me. There is no way I should allow myself lose money because he is attracted to me. I just need to keep my distance from him: no more private plane rides and such. I opened the second bottle of the mini red wine and downed it. Once my skin had softened from the therapeutic bath, my body felt relaxed. I put my bathrobe on and went into the bedroom. I did a belly flop on the plush bed and fell into a catatonic state.

***

The blasting sound of classical Italian music woke me from my sleep. As my eyes slowly opened, I felt the wind whipping my dark curls across my face. I was sitting in the passenger seat of what appeared to be a 1965 Corvette convertible with the top down, my head resting on the door, but hanging halfway out of the car. Turning my head slowly, I felt stiffness in my neck, but it faded once I saw that the person behind the wheel was Pablo. "Where are we?" I shouted to him. "Italy. We're on our way to the Marisa Cuomo winery. It's just off the Amalfi Coast. We should be there in about half an hour. Go back to sleep. I'll wake you when we arrive." He cranked up Renato Carne's *Tu Vuò Fá L'Americano* and kept driving like a maniac. The sky shimmered with a sunset hue as the clouds danced. Pablo kept singing and smoking a pipe, acting like Ricky, knowing every word. The car slowed as it entered a tunnel, navigating a sharp turn. Pablo got out, circled to my side, and opened the door. "Let's watch the sunset, beautiful," he said with a reassuring smile. I grabbed his hand and stepped out of the car. As we moved toward the small open space near the bushy edge of the scenic overlook, the sky suddenly darkened to gray, and the water turned a blood-red hue. I slowly backed away from the bloody water's edge toward the car. At that moment, Pablo's eyes also turned red. He stood there still, smiling, with eyes as red as vampires in their early stages in the movie Twilight, but I wasn't afraid. Mesmerized, I slowly approached him. Now, face-to-face, I saw that he truly was a vampire. He tenderly caressed my cheek with a kiss. Hypnotized by his charming gaze, he bit into my neck and began sucking profusely. However, it felt like a crick in your neck rather than a stabbing pain. My eyes began to open as slowly as elevator doors to reality.

"Yo, I have the wildest dreams," I said out loud—nothing uncommon, however, just an ordinary crazy visit to Dreamland.

I had three missed calls from LC and texts from Will and Jessie. Will wanted me to know it would be a longer night than he initially thought. I already figured it would be, which is why our anniversary weekend was rescheduled. Jessie texted to let me know she was in town and asked if I could come to a private event Pablo was hosting in Harlem tonight.

"I thought he was in jail?" I said out loud. After that recent dream, I was not desperate to be in the company of Pablo tha Picasso, but I didn't have anything else going on tonight.

"Didn't come all the way to my hometown to be sitting up in my room like Brandy, so why not?" I said to myself. I replied to Will about going out with J tonight. I texted J to send me the deets for the so-called jailbird's event.

The driver pulled up to the address Jessie had given me. He got out and opened the door for me. I checked the address on the building and the address Jessie sent to me to ensure they matched, as it looked rather vacant.

"Are you sure this is the right place, Miss?" the driver asked, looking perplexed. Walking up the building's stairs, I realized it was abandoned when I saw a red-and-white X on the door. I texted Jessie to make sure I was at the right place. She texted back

YEP, WALK THROUGH THE DOOR AND GO UP THE
STAIRS ON YOUR RIGHT.

There wasn't a soul walking or talking in the downstairs area. As I walked up the stairs on the right, I pinched myself to ensure I wasn't dreaming. There was a long, creepy hallway of doors when I got to the top. You've got to be kidding me! Why didn't she tell me which door it would be? None, as far as I could see, had numbers or signage. I called her back to see which door, but she didn't pick up. I entered the door closest to me. When I opened it, there was a party of a lifetime going on behind it. The entire loft was filled with a diverse group of people. They were dancing and talking, but mostly dancing. There had to be over one hundred people in there. I walked around the perimeter to find Jessie standing by the makeshift bar, holding two double-shot glasses. She handed one to me and said,

"Do you know what today is? It's your anniversary!"

"And I'm standing here with you instead of with Will. What's wrong with this picture?"

"Absolutely nothing as far as I can see. Love you, Genie!" she replied. She smacked a kiss on my cheek and took her shot. I smiled, did the same to her, and took my shot.

"So, they're serving the cheap liquor tonight. No wonder everybody's lit." She grabbed the glasses and set them on the bar.

"No worries, I have the good, good at our table." I followed her up into the loft area. Pablo was sitting in a roped-off section, talking with some very influential-looking men in tailored suits — investors, I assumed. The party vibe downstairs had dimmed a bit. I sat in the lounge area next to Pablo's VIP section. Jessie sat with me, filling me in on how the NYPD pulled Pablo over for dark-tinted windows, and someone in his entourage had drugs in the car, so they arrested everyone.

"Yeah, girl. Here we go with this street life shit that black music artists always seem to succumb to. Thank God it wasn't Pablo with the drugs on him…." I listened to her unconsciously, with my mind stuck on the crazy dreams of Pablo I'd been having lately. I wanted to stay as far away from the green-eyed monster as possible. Jessie's voice finally interrupted my deep thought. "So, is that a yes or a no? Genie. Genie!" She nudged my leg. "I'm sorry. What were you asking?"

"Do you want another drink?" She looked puzzled.

    THE DREAM LIFE

"Oh. No thanks. I need to be fresh for my shoot tomorrow. So, I am not going to stay long."

"You working on your anniversary getaway?" She folded her arms in a distasteful fashion.

"You know work never sleeps. Same as me being here with you, instead of somewhere with my man." She laughed.

"Whatever. You know you only came to see Pablo."

"That's not even how I do business J, and you know that."

"Be honest, G. He's sexy as hell. I would give it a ride if I were you. Forget that contract!"

"And that's the difference between you and me. I'm strictly business, and you're strictly dickly." We stared at each other briefly before bursting into laughter. I glanced at his VIP area, and he was looking directly at me. I kept looking at him as if his stare cast a trance over me from across the room, just like in my dream. I could see him whispering something to the guy beside him while still maintaining eye contact with me.

"Here he comes, girl. I'm going to get you a drink anyway. Be right back."

"J, I don't need another one. Jessie..." She kept walking over to the bar. Pablo sat down beside me.

"Well, isn't this a beautiful surprise?" he said, smiling cheek to cheek.

"A surprise for both of us. Nice welcome home party."

"Oh, that's cold." His face fell.

"Just a joke. Don't take it personal."

He quietly looked at me. "Why is it that every time you're in my presence, I can't see nothing but you? Let me take you out to dinner."

I rolled my eyes. "Pablo, haven't we discussed this?" "Yeah, yeah, yeah. I know you got a man and all, but you're here instead of with him, so...." He stroked his chin as if he were trying to solve a puzzle.

"I'm here with my girl. I'm not the type to need to be under someone's thumb to know they're still around. We're both hardworking professionals; grueling hours come with the territory."

"Well, that Princeton pledge of a hard-working couple doesn't explain how a man could have a queen of your caliber at some lame loft party instead of planning a weekend off the coast of Italy. Sometimes you just have to put what should be first, first." I was startled by his intuitive words. Jessie returned carrying two shots. I grabbed one and downed it immediately.

Pablo turned to Jessie and said, "I gotta get back to networking. Jessie, I have a vision for the video for my new single. Let's talk soon, cool?"

"Yes, tomorrow I have some free time around two. I'll call you," she said, checking the calendar on her phone.

"Great. Ms. Rae Roman, as always, it's been a pleasure, but I must get back to greasing these palms. Hey Jessie, Ms. Rae would be a great leading lady in this new joint. It's a banger just like her." I gave him a slight nod.

"What was that about?" she asked. I changed the subject.

"Guess who I briefly chatted with today?"

"Who?"

"Guess!"

"Ummm....? I give up, who?"

"Boss."

"For real? How did that happen?"

THE DREAM LIFE

"I texted him to be my date for a show on Broadway."
"Is he still bitter?"
"As a lemon.

CHAPTER 8

My Dream Job

I awoke the following day to a breakfast platter lying beside me with a note that read,

PLEASE BELIEVE ME WHEN I SAY,
I'D RATHER BE EATING BREAKFAST BETWEEN YOUR LEGS THAN
GOING TO WORK. THANK YOU FOR LOVING ME AND BEING SO
UNDERSTANDING.

Will was already headed to the office after arriving late last night. "Damn. That deal must be a beast," I said to myself. I decided to help at the shoot today since I didn't have Will here to cuddle the day away. "Might as well do something productive with the day," I mumbled. LC was lucky to know me so well that she knew I'd always traveled with an on-the-go camera.

When I arrived at the shoot, I was surprised to see Cindy among the models. She was the first girl that Will seriously dated after we broke up during our freshman year in college. She recognized me from the look on her face. In Will's opinion, their relationship never worked out because she always felt inferior to me.

The connection between Will and me had always been dynamic. She would hate it when we'd call each other now and then to catch up. It was almost like we knew we would get back together. We just had some self-discovery to do. Cindy walked over to one of the models and started to whisper. I know she was talking about me because she was looking directly at me.

Roy, the Cosmo coordinator working the set, came over and started discussing the shoot's intentions and ideas with me. I had worked with him on a previous layout for the magazine about a year ago. He was down-to-earth and fun to work alongside.I suggested that he take some photos out in the elements. He agreed. I introduced myself to the models.

"Attention. Attention. Hello everyone. I'm Rae Roman. We're going to have a good time today. If anyone has any suggestions, you can keep them to yourself." I paused. All of them looked at me with blank stares.

"Okay, tough crowd. I'm often interested in the models' vision of the shoot's direction. When it's all said and done, it is your image that's displayed to the public. Roy also discussed the overall intention: to focus on everyday fashion and fun. We will also get some shots outside. Any questions?"

Cindy immediately asked, "Do you have the qualifications to work for a company of this magnitude? You don't have that professional look, if you know what I mean." Her terrible, fake British accent sent a chill down my spine.

My left eyebrow involuntarily lifted. "And who are you again?" I acted as if I didn't remember her, even though I knew that bitch.

"My name is just as irrelevant to you as that knock-off Gucci fanny pack you have on your waist." Roy came to my defense. "If you think you're about to talk to Rae Roman like that and stay on this set, honey... think again!" She looked at him in shock, her mouth gaping.

"You can pick up your chin and head back to whatever corner you were working last night."

"No worries, Roy. She can stay. I have the perfect picture with her in mind." I couldn't believe she was still salty with me after all these years. She had no idea she was one of many who couldn't come between what Will and I shared. I could not wait to tell Will about his ex's ratchet behavior on my set. Before we began, I stepped outside to clear my mind of the unnecessary negative energy I had just been subjected to. The door opened. It was Roy.

"You okay, Rae?"

"Are you kidding me? I eat chicas like her for breakfast. I also have a perfect vision for the shots I will use of Little Ms. Unprofessional today. Do you get my drift?" I winked at him. He grinned mischievously. "I got you, girl. Teach her ass how to put some R-E-S-P-E-C-T on your name, honey..." he said, gesturing with hair flips and snaps. Roy left and came right back to say, "And we're ready to get started whenever you

   THE DREAM LIFE

are." I didn't use Cindy in a single shot. At the end of the shoot, the LC company informed her agent that she would be prohibited from any of my bookings going forward due to her hostile harassment. Later that week, our Rights and Ethics department spoke with the casting producer at Cosmopolitan to report her unprofessional behavior. Knowing that all the creative directors and casting agents for high-fashion brands and magazines are in cahoots, I expected a domino effect. Checkmate, bitch. That will be a valuable way to demonstrate my qualifications in this business to her. Being able to call the shots and take names was a perk of my dream job.

When I returned to the hotel, Will was in the bathroom on the phone. It sounded like he was going back and forth with someone. I sat on the bed and took off my shoes. I heard him turn on the shower. I took off my clothes to join him. As I opened the large glass door and stepped into the steam-filled space, I paused, taking a moment to admire every detail of his ripped physique. I missed his warm, buttery skin melting into mine.

"Hello, my honey dip," I said softly. Will damn near jumped out of his skin.

"Rae! What the hell are you sneaking up on me like a thief for?"

"Sorry. Just trying to steal some dick before my flight tonight."

"Do you have to? Can't you stay just one more night?"

"Yes. We have a wedding that the agency booked months ago."

"Well, in that case." Will lifted me and anchored me against the tile. I weaved my arms and legs around his neck and waist. He instantly grew as I gave him soft kisses on his top chakra. Will was the best 'tease me, please me, and make me want it more' kind of partner.

"Put me down," I demanded. When I jumped down, his love stick whacked me right in the vajayjay. I took the soap and started to bathe him. He closed his eyes and relaxed. As I got lower, I dropped to my knees and took him into my mouth. He began to moan. Stroking his sack with the bar of soap, I took more and more of him inside my warm mouth. Deeper and thicker, he swelled. He began to lose his stance. At the brink of his climax, I stood up and said my turn. Will picked me up and threw me up on his shoulders. As I floated above the cloudy steam shower, I closed my eyes and enjoyed the passion he was bringing to the table. After several rounds of pleasuring each other in the shower, we collapsed on top of the luxurious Egyptian cotton comforter.

The sky was painted a deep tangerine orange. Fields of grapevines stretched as far as the eye could see. A white-haired woman stood in a vineyard, filling a jug with the biggest grapes I've ever tasted in my life. A few feet away, a gentleman wore a large straw hat. I stepped closer to him to see who he was, but he turned around before I reached him. "Are you ready to go smash some grapes?"

"Pablo! Where are we?" "Only where the best grapes in the world are grown." Knowing immediately that it was a dream, I forced myself to wake up. Will was staring at me.

"Who the fuck is Pablo?" he asked.

CHAPTER 9

Lucid Dream Trap

"**G**ene Rae, the best part of my life began when I had you. You know you almost took my life as I tried to bring you into the world the natural way, right?"

As far as I can remember, every birthday started with my mother reminding me how I almost killed her coming into this world.

"Yes, Mom. How can I forget? You tell me every year," I said flatly.

"But I would go through that pain over and over again just to have a daughter as intelligent, phenomenal, and loving as

the one I have. Oh, and let's not forget the beauty of the gods."
I listened quietly to her. She would go on like this every year,
so it was best not to interrupt, as it would only make her speech
longer. I've never been big on birthdays. To me, it was just
another day. Birthdays are simply reminders that you're getting
closer and closer to the inevitable fate of life, not as you once
knew it, when your body would move before your mind could
tell it to. Death is always lurking among us; that's a fact. I once
thought of life as a lucid dream trap that repeats itself lifetime
after lifetime. So many questions still have no answers. So
many opportunities and experiences that one will no longer be
able to live out when the untimely end comes knocking at your
door. I pulled myself out of my morbid thoughts to focus back
on my mother's expressions of love for me, though I know I
gave her many concerns over my years of living.

"But with all that being said, Gene Rae, you are the
brightest star on the darkest night. I love you beyond the
galaxies!"

"I love you too, Mom!"

"Don't forget to check the mail. Your package should be
on the way soon."

"Guess what? I got it today."
The traditional birthday card with the number of dollars
matching my age, and one extra dollar to grow on. A custom
handed down by my grandparents.

"Thank you for the package, Mama. Kiss Dad for me."

"One more thing before I let you go. Those eggs of yours
are not getting any younger, honey." *Damn,* I thought I had
escaped the constant reminder that my eggs are just as old as I
am for the umpteenth time. She continued. "And neither am I.

You and William should go ahead and get married so I can enjoy grandparenthood before I get any older. You hear me?" Of course, that's the priority in childbearing for me, getting to it before my parents' youthfulness is all gone.

"Okay, Mama, I'll try to push a few out before you're all decrepit and gray..."

"I know you're not trying to get smart with me, Gene Rae? And gray who and gray where? You know I plan to dye until I die." She laughed and hung up on me.

Will seemed to have a stick still up his butt when I spoke with him. He knows how lucid my dreams are, and that calling Pablo's name meant nothing. For some reason, Will didn't believe me.

"If you care for someone you are working with," he said, raising air quotes around "working," "so intensely that you bring them into your dreams... I'm not sure about that, Rae." Now, whenever I mention I'm with Jessie or at work, he assumes I'm canoodling with Pablo. Oh well, the money is green, and he'll eventually get over it.

I was walking down the stairs to go into my darkroom. As I searched my playlist for Nina's version of *Ne me quitte pas,* I got a call from LC.

"And how might I help you today, Ms. Calloway?"

"Don't I get a hello?"

"Hello. How might I help you today, Ms. Calloway?"

"Rae, cut out the smartass tone. Have you decided whether you'll be attending the company's annual Thanksgiving trip? Is it in Dubai this year?

"LC, you know my mother has been on my neck about coming home for Thanksgiving, and I have already told her that Will and I are planning to come. I've already missed a couple of years due to work and company trips, so I can't disappoint her this year."

"I hear ya! Glad my parents never wanted me for longer than it took to conceive me."

"Is that why you always host company trips during holidays? Because we are your family, LC?" I said sarcastically.

"Girl, you're already abreast of this information. Are you trying to hurt my feelings?"

"I was just joking, don't be so sensitive, LC. See, this is why you need to find a man with some good values and grown kids."

"Rae, what do I look like, trotting behind some old grandpa with my fine self?" Even though LC was Italian as gelato, I could hear every black mama, aunt, sister, and cousin I knew in her tone.

Lauren Calloway, born Lorinza Cavallaro, was raised by her mother's best friend, Ms. Lizzy, and her husband. Her mother abandoned her responsibilities when LC was just ten years old, much like her father had done on her first birthday. It was the only story she could remember her mother endlessly retelling her.

"He left me high and dry on your first birthday to be with the wife and family he already had."

She reconnected with her father over the years but never saw her mom again. She once told me that this was why she never cared to get married or have children. She's too afraid of being

   THE DREAM LIFE

the wife at home who gets cheated on or the pregnant mistress no one wants to claim.

After I hung up the phone with her, I started searching for Nina's playlist as I headed into my darkroom to develop prints from the Cosmo shoot. Ironically, it started with "HERE COMES THE SUN." Listening to Nina's sultry voice always made me wish I had pursued my somewhat singing career when Boss gave me the chance. Oh well, maybe in the next lifetime.

Later that day, I got a call from Will. I was surprised. Lately, he'd been in his feelings about me working with Pablo, oh, and me calling Pablo's name in my sleep.

"Hey, my King!" I answered. "Hey, Queen. What are you up to?"

"Oh, nothing. Just assembling some prints I developed earlier? Is everything okay?"

"Yes. Is everything okay with you?"

"Just dandy. Now, is everything okay with us?"

"Why wouldn't they be, Rae?"

"Well, lately, you've been up in arms about my working with Pablo...." I paused to hear his response.

He interjected. "And calling his name in your dreams...."

"Right, so I just wanna make sure we're cool. Please stop giving me the third degree when I tell you I'm with J or working with Pablo. Okay?"

"You're right, my love. I have been a bit salty. But imagine if I were calling out a woman's name while lying next to you, and you heard me. Wouldn't you be a bit hesitant about that said woman if she were my colleague?"

"You are unquestionably right, but once you told me it was nothing, I would let it be."

"Okay, okay, I've been holding this over your head out of jealousy. He gets to spend so much time with you, but that's my fault, too. I just thought," he stopped. "You're right, babe. I'm sorry. I love you, Gene Rae Roman. I trust you."

"Great. So now that's settled. Thanksgiving?"

"Oh no, don't even start that shit."

Will had a firm belief against celebrating Thanksgiving Day because of his Native American descendants. Will's father's great-great-grandparents were from the Seneca tribe. Growing up, his parents made him and his brother attend events on reservations to instill traditions, hoping their ancestors' legacies and stories of triumph would continue to be taught to future generations. Will's mother ended up having an affair with her Jewish boss and divorced his father, soon after converting them to Judaism. Will's ideologies seemed to conform to his stepdad's ideals as he grew older. However, his conviction about Thanksgiving never let up.

"Will, when it comes to this holiday, it's solely about family, food, and football. Not terrorizing or colonizing. Plus, this is my mom's favorite holiday, and I have already told her we would be there."

"I thought her favorite holiday was Christmas, or was it Halloween?"

"Okay, okay, she loves holidays, so?"

"In any case, she still hates me. I'm sure she won't miss my presence."

"Will, that's so juvenile of you to hold a grudge with my mother still all these years later. She only wanted what was best for me and my future at the time, like any mom would. Let it go already."

"Well, I guess your mom and I are both juveniles because she still talks to me with disdain in her voice."

"She got over that years ago. Why can't you?"

"The bigger question is, how could you ever let something like that fade from your memory, Rae?"

"Are you kidding me, Will? That experience will never fade from my memory. Listen, I understand this is a tough one for you. I played it cool for years with your beliefs, but now we are grown-ups. If we want to spend our lives together, we have to compromise. This year, it is vital to my mom that we be there, and…."

"All right, all right, I'll go," he said woefully.

"You will! Oh great! Thank you. I know she will be so excited we are coming."

"We'll see about that." Will huffed.

Dream Chasing

J essie and I flew out to LA for the week to do some press for Pablo. Tony arranged a car to pick us up from the airport.

"Where exactly are we going, J?" The driver was taking us far up the 101.

"Girl, these artists," she said, fidgeting through her oversized tote bag. "You know how they have to try and fit the successful artist profile, or maybe I should say, seemingly successful artist profile. They rented a mansion out in the Bu. So, we will be staying there." She gave me a side-eye because she knew I wasn't pleased with this information.

"Don't even give me that look, Jessie. You already know I can't."

"Can't or won't?" Her comeback was sharp, but I didn't see the difference. I didn't counter her question. I got on my iPad and searched for a hotel or an Airbnb. To my misfortune, everything was booked all over LA. Come to find out, there was a three-day concert called Woodstock 2K. Pablo was hosting a party for the show tonight at a venue in Malibu. Now I had no choice but to stay at Pablo's rented mansion for this trip.

"Damn. Everything is booked! Everywhere," I grunted. "J, how come you didn't book a place for us like you usually do for these work events?"

"Didn't make any sense to book a place if we have to be trailing Pablo around. It makes more sense to stay with him for no funds in a big-ass mansion. Don't worry; you won't even see him. Come on, G. I thought we were chasing this dream together?"

We arrived at the enormous Mediterranean-style mansion. Two beefy guards were standing at the door. As I lollygagged, not anticipating having to stay the weekend under the same roof as Pablo, I heard Jessie having words with the man at the door.

"Call him. He'll tell you."

"What's the problem, J?" She turned to me and said,

"Nothing. You know how these security guards try to outdo themselves to get the perks of the lifestyle." She turned to them and said, "What are y'all waiting on? You know what? I'll do it." Within a minute after Jessie made the phone call,

Pablo's short, stubby manager opened the door, holding a serving platter of shots.

"Ladies, ladies, please come in! Welcome to Pablo's winning weekend in the Bu! This weekend the answer to everything is yes! Bring y'all sexy selves on in here!"

"Oh, so the welcome wagon is in full effect, huh, Tony?"

"Sorry about the security, but they're just doing their job. Pablo went to Rodeo Drive with some of the entourage. He should be back momentarily. Find a room you like, have a snack and another drink, and make yourselves at home."

"Okay, thanks, Tone…." Jessie said, already piling fruit on a small plate from the buffet table.

We went upstairs to find a room before the entourage took them all, but little did we know, they had already claimed them.

"No worries. We can just find someone who will share their room with us." She would have been dead with my sharp glance if looks could kill.

"See, this is why I don't mix business and pleasure. Now we have to share rooms! Oh no! I…"

"Genie, before you sweat out your press, just know this won't happen again."

"That's for certain. Did you tell Pablo we were staying here, too?"

"I did, and he knows it's all business. I'm sure it's just a case of THE ENTOURAGE." She made air quotes with her hands.

"The same thing that got him locked up, THE ENTOURAGE."

"Listen to you sounding like a possessive Mum." Jessie's time living in London occasionally surfaced in her accent. She

   THE DREAM LIFE

walked over to me and wrapped her arms around me as I stood there holding my suitcases.

"Give me these. Are we here to work? Yes, but… We are also here to enjoy life with every breath we take." She would always break out the YOLO mantras whenever I got too serious. I cracked a slight smirk and said, "Okay, okay! Let's go tan by the pool."

"Now you're speaking my language," she said as she threw my suitcases aside.

"Hey! That's heirloom Louie luggage, girl. Watch how you handle them, please."

"Damn girl. My bad. We for sure need to get you another drink or two to loosen up."

Jessie and I were at the pool, two drinks in, when we noticed that Pablo and the entourage had returned. There were only five men and three women. They headed straight for the food and drinks, then came over and started getting into the pool. One of the men did a cannonball with his clothes still on. He got out, stripped down to his underwear, and then hopped back in. "What sense did that make?" Jessie said aloud. The server greeted us and asked, "Can I get you all a refill?" Pablo appeared from nowhere before we could respond, saying,

"Yes, bring over a bottle for the ladies," he paused and looked at Jessie. "A bowl of maraschino cherries for Jessie, right?" She nodded. "And let's get a double round of shots for everyone. Thanks!" The hosts said, "Right away, sir."
The sky turned violet and amber. Jessie and I had spent what felt like hours strategizing ways to improve Pablo's broadband.

"If we can get his fans and those who would never listen to his music to connect with him personally, it will help solidify who he is as an entertainer. Take social media, for example. It makes people think they know celebrities personally. Even though they don't, it keeps them interested and wanting more. Maybe he can start a vlog," Jessie said, trying to devise a master plan to boost Pablo's career.

"We've been at this for hours. I'm telling you, J, humanitarianism is where he needs to focus his mindset. Social media is powerful, but it's a slippery slope that lacks substance. I'm not saying don't use it, but today's youth need to be inspired not only by those who can rap about money, sex, and drugs, but also by those who will help them break free from their stagnant mentality and grow their generational wealth and health."

"I love you, Genie, so much for wanting to push the empowerment of communities to advance the world's mindset, but did you learn anything from the rise and fall of the Black Panther Party? These record companies don't give two shits about raising the vibrations on health and wealth."

"Well, it's a new dawn. Right here and right now, let's make a declaration to guide Pablo into being perceived as an artist who will make a positive mark with his music and actions." I stood up with excitement, as if I were giving a toast.

"Okay, but it's still up to Pablo to decide his fate."

"Is it, J? Is it really? Just think of all these artists out here being controlled. They are told how to look, eat, sing, dress, when to sleep, etc. Their record labels influence their every single move."

"But Pablo is independent." I threw my glass in the air.

"Exactly! Cheers!" She clinked my glass, not understanding the message I was trying to convey.

"I don't get it, but okay." I took her champagne glass away.

"Okay, you can't be that inebriated already," I said, looking her eye to eye. It was clear she was tipsy.

"My sweet, dearest friend, other than Tony, no one is guiding Pablo's career except you. You can steer this boat toward great things and unlock a brighter future. Besides, Tony doesn't seem to be as legit a manager as he needs to be to get his career to more influential heights." The light finally went off in her head.

"Oh, I get it! Become more than his publicist."

"Haven't you realized you are already more than just his publicist, J?" I gave her the champagne back with a wink. She clinked the glass on mine to fully acknowledge where this opportunity could go. She had that hustler's glow in her eyes, the look she gets when ideas dance around in her head.

One of Pablo's songs started playing. It was one I liked. He performed this song at the beginning of his show to get the crowd hyped. I stood up and began swaying my hips to the beat.

Jessie said, "Whoa. It looks like things are starting to heat up over there." I turned to see the girls with their tops off frolicking in the pool. The guys' eyes were bugged out like cartoon characters. One blonde girl was twerking and bouncing her butt like a pro. Another purple-haired girl came up behind her and started grinding on Blondie's butt. She slowly began sliding Blondie's thong off on purpose. Then we saw her go down and kiss each cheek back and forth. It wasn't long before the last girl in the group joined in, kissing Blondie. Everyone at the pool was watching, including Jessie and me. The men were shouting obscenities.

"Eat her ass…."

"Go down on her…."

"Hey, ladies, can I join your freak feast….?"

It was all typical entourage and groupie behavior. Pablo came out of the house looking refreshed and dressed. Jessie drunkenly slurred, "Heeeey P, we've been talking about youuu. Where have you been?"

"On the phone with my mom. She's not doing too great. You ladies can come inside and have some food. The chef has prepared an exquisite feast for us before we head out to the event tonight. We are heading out around ten, right, Jessie?"

"Yep, it's not far from here. Rae and I had trouble finding an available room for our stay here in this fancy mansion..." Jessie paused and hiccupped. "It's just so darn big…" She put her hand up to her mouth and hiccupped again.

"Excuse me." Whenever Jessie began the hiccups, she was maxed out.

"No problem, you ladies can stay in my suite. I'll find a couch or somewhere around here to crash. I'm so tired right now I can sleep standing up."

"Paaablooo…" Jessie dragged his name out. "That's so sweet, P! Isn't he the sweetest, G?" He turned and walked towards me. I stood there awkwardly, awaiting his Mac Daddy charm.

"Have you been enjoying your stay so far, Ms. Roman?" Pablo shifted his gaze towards me.

"Yes, thank you."

"Let me know if you need anything, and we'll find a way to get it to you."

"Heeey, what about meeee?"

"Jessie, you know you take care of us all. So, you know whatever you say goes," Pablo said, smiling.

Jessie and I looked at each other. I winked at her. It proved that Jessie was a deciding factor in guiding his career in a positive direction. If she played her cards right, this could be a grand opportunity for her.

We abandoned the poolside freak fest after the guy who jumped in earlier, fully dressed, was now without underwear, getting his manhood manipulated by Blondie on the pool steps.

After the event, even more people returned to the mansion. I heard one of the chefs say, "The midnight feast is now being served. It will be available in the outdoor dining areas." Jessie and I made our way to the feast to soak up all the alcohol we had been drinking. The food was the perfect cure for our drunken bellies. I grabbed one of the sliders and told her I was going upstairs to relax.

"Cool. Black shirt at twelve o'clock keeps eyeing me, so I'm going to hang around for a bit." I discreetly look in the twelve o'clock direction. Brother was fine. I gave her a thumbs up and said, "Tits up! Good night."

CHAPTER 11

Pipe Dreams

As I walked up the stairs to get my Louie out of the room Jessie had thrown them into, I saw Pablo and Tony in the upstairs foyer talking in very low voices with intense looks. "Hi, gentlemen." They immediately broke apart, as if they were hiding something. They just stood there without acknowledging me. I gave an awkward "okay" and then asked Pablo to show me the suite he mentioned earlier. "Sure, Rae, and I'll come to grab your luggage." I gave him a yawning "Thank you."

"Which room is it in?" he asked. I walk ahead of him, scavenging for my luggage.

"Good question. Early today seems so long ago now. I think it was down this hall," I told him.

We walked the long, checkered hallway, opening and closing doors as we went. It was the very last door at the end of the hall. When I opened the door, there stood Blondie from earlier, fully nude, accompanied by two girls and two guys. Blondie was doing a line of coke off the dick of one of the guys in the entourage. Everyone in the room was sexually attached in some way. I stood there like a deer in headlights. Pablo did too.

"Hey, pretty girl. Y'all looking to join?"

"Yeah, sexy. Come join this pipe party. I have enough to share with three."

I refocused on the original plan and saw Louie still sprawled where Jessie had thrown him. I quickly walked over to pick him up. I put Jessie's duffel on my shoulder and grabbed my suitcases. Pablo grabbed them away from me as I was leaving the room.

"Wow. Are your parties always so…? So…?" I tried to find the right word without sounding judgmental, but he interrupted.

"Buckwild and freaky?" he implied. I shook my head, yes, still wearing a stunned facial expression. "No. I can't even tell you who they were. Different people are coming out of the woodwork these days." We walked around the corner. He opened the door I presumed was his suite, but it turned out to be an elevator door. He inserted a keycard and entered code 1912. The door opened into a small foyer, with two French doors leading to what appeared to be an apartment big enough for a small family.

"This is lovely," I said unintentionally out loud.

"Not as lovely as you." I looked at him, tilted my head, and smiled.

"Here's the key for the elevator. Just put it in and press the code 1912. You can return the keycard to Tony or one of the staff before you leave." We shared a moment of silence.

"Well, enjoy the rest of your night," he let out a loud yawn. "Man, I'm exhausted. I think I'm going to call it a night. Do you need anything before I go?"

"No, I'm good, thanks." As he reached the door for the elevator, I shouted out. "Pablo, wait!"

"Yes, Rae, what is it?"

"If you see Jessie, give it to her so she will have access up," I said, handing him the keycard back. "Also, let her know how to get up here. And let her know I got her bag. Never mind, I'll just text her."

"Okay, well, I'll get out of here so you can do your thang. Goodnight, Ms. Rae Roman."

"Pablo...."

"Yes, Rae." He turned back with much anticipation as if I would ask him to read me a bedtime story.

"Thanks again for the suite."

"A suite for my sweet," he said. I shook my head and smiled.

It was after three a.m. when I crashed on the bed after steaming in the suite's enormous shower. As I closed my eyes and drifted off to Dreamland, I remembered I had forgotten to text Jessie. I walked into the living room area to get my phone.

Just then, I saw Pablo coming through the French doors. He had changed into what appeared to be loungewear. He was wearing basketball shorts and a golf tee. Through his shorts, I could attest by his dick print that his manhood was also constructed well.

I stood still as he came toward me, walking authoritatively.

"Did you forget something, Pablo?"

He grabbed the belt on my robe and pulled me into him.

"Yeah, this." He kissed me. There was no space, no air, nothing between us. The kiss started softly and gently, as if he were asking for my permission just by kissing me. He wasn't waiting for a yes or no—maybe a pushback. When that didn't happen, the kiss deepened into a passionate, tongue-fighting battle between us. We collapsed onto the couch without pulling away. I straddled him and plunged my tongue further into his mouth. He palmed my bare ass under my terry cloth robe. The atmosphere was thick with desire, filling the room. As I slowly traced my hands over his chest and down his abs, I could feel his blood rushing to his hardening arousal. I kept going to get hands-on evidence of the weight of what was growing inside his shorts. For a few seconds, our lips parted as my phone rang, breaking our steamy necking. He grabbed my face to reconnect, but the phone kept ringing and ringing. I thought it was probably Jessie. I was supposed to be texting her. How did I end up here? The phone kept ringing. I didn't want to stop. I wanted to experience the hype around Mr. Pablo Picasso myself.

The phone kept ringing. I crawled over Pablo's shoulders to grab my phone on the side table, my nether region sitting right in his face. He parted my robe and started licking at my southern lips. I collapsed and dropped the phone that wouldn't stop ringing.

Jessie and the black-shirt guy who lingered around her at the party burst through the French doors. Pablo and I scattered and gathered ourselves. I adjusted my robe, and he adjusted the prominent bulge in his shorts.

"Knock much!" I said to them. Jessie busted out laughing.

"Hahahaha!! Girl, my bad! I was trying to call first! Why didn't you guys put a sock on the door?" We locked eyes, and I'm sure she recognized my facial expression AS GET THE HELL OUT NOW!

Jessie turned around and told the guy still standing at the door, "Let's go back downstairs and get in the jacuzzi. Just let me grab my swimsuit. Meet me down there..." The guy quietly left. Jessie tiptoed over to retrieve her bag as if she hadn't already interrupted what was about to go down between Pablo and me. After she disappeared, the elephant in the room stood tall and wide. "Well, that took an unexpected turn." I turned to him and asked,

"What turn were you intending this to take?"

"Not where it was going, but they're gone now. Let's get back to where we were headed," he said, coming closer. I stood there with my feet riveted to the floor.

He wrapped his arm around me and picked me up. I still couldn't move. I felt as though the sleep demon was sitting on my motor functions. Pablo whisked me away to the bed and began kissing me. He flipped me over and stripped my robe

                    THE DREAM LIFE

off, exposing my naked body. I felt something long and heavy lying between my cheeks.

I awoke alone in an unrecognizable place. Then a flashback hit me of the night before. I reached for my phone on the side table but couldn't find it. I peeled myself off the bed and saw that it was nowhere nearby. Walking into the living room, Jessie's luggage was gone. I located my phone on the floor. I listened to Jessie's message telling me she was bunking with the guy from the party. A voice message from Will said, "Hi, my love. I have a big deal to close by the end of Thanksgiving week…." I didn't listen to the rest of the message because I already knew where that story was headed. Will had a huge business deal that would dampen our plans for the upcoming holiday. Big surprise.

Trying to gather my thoughts on what happened the night before, I sat on the bed and contemplated if what I assumed happened actually happened, or was it all a dream?

CHAPTER 12

Not in my wildest dreams

When I exited the suite, I noticed fresh orchids on the foyer table that weren't there the night before. There was a note that had 'Rae' written on the front, underlined. I eased the message open with anticipation.

ROSES ARE RED,
SOME ARE WHITE.
LIKE THE ORCHIDS YOU LOVE,
YOU TOO ARE MY FAVORITE TYPE.
-PABLO

I was baffled. So, it wasn't a dream? My thoughts became blurred. I went back into the bedroom to look for signs of lovemaking. I didn't see a used condom wrapper. Not in my wildest dreams would I have had sex unprotected. I didn't notice any stains on the sheets. I steadily tried to convince myself that I did not get entangled with Mr. Green Eyes. Get it together, girl. You are smarter than that. I reassured myself that I was not the type to hook up with a client, especially a rapper, in my little pep talk. HE'S YOUR CLIENT! HE'S A RAPPER! COME ON, RAE. ARE YOU KIDDING ME? OF COURSE, NOTHING HAPPENED. I phoned J and told her to come to the suite ASAP to put my mind at ease.

When she entered, I could tell that she hadn't been to sleep by the dark shades, messy hair, raspy voice, and the same clothes as yesterday.

"Hey, girl. How was your night?"

She started with, "Girl!" and paused. I knew then it was a situation.

"Did you and that guy you were hitched to downstairs come in this suite last night?" I asked her without giving her any information that could incriminate me.

She looked confused. "Uh, no. But I did see Pablo, and he told me where I could find you and my luggage. This morning, I needed to get my charger, so he came up here to get it for me. Did you see the lovely orchids Pablo delivered to you? He asked me what your favorite type of flower was last night. I told him white orchids. But not the cheap supermarket type. The type you get from a decent florist shop." Jessie continued to talk, and I tuned her out, thinking, great, that means I didn't sleep with him.

I sighed with relief. That dream was so lucid. I could feel my vagina throbbing as I relived the moments we shared in the dream. In the past, Will and I had many issues with fidelity because I was too stubborn to commit solely to him, and he would also let Cindy bounce on his dick whenever she wanted. We both knew we were too young and naive at the time, so we didn't let small hookups with others tear us apart. What we had was more solid than some casual fling. There was always an understanding that we had to use full discretion and protection when dating others to avoid unwanted consequences. Safe sex and regular testing were priorities.

However, we were more serious about our commitment and relationship this time. We agreed to share our intimacy and passion with no one else. We had both gotten the playing games and sleeping around era out of our system. At least, this is what I wanted to believe for myself.

Jessie was still schmoozing about how enormous the black shirt guy's shlong was. "Girl, I thought my appendix was going to rupture." She finally went quiet. "You okay, G? You must be in your head about something. Or is it someone?" I gave her a look that said she was right.

"I knew it! Mr. Dreamy and those eyes getting to you? Isn't he?"

"Girl, ain't nobody thinking about Pablo," I lied. "But I was thinking, while we are in LA, that maybe Pablo could go to an inner-city school and talk to the youth about staying in school and take them some school supplies. You know, a way to boost his image and name. But just a thought. I don't want to step on your toes, Ms. PR. I'm just here to capture the moments. I'm about to get ready to head out."

"That's not a bad idea, Genie. I'll run it by him. Maybe we can get it in today before the show tonight."

"Wait! What do you mean head out?"

"Head out, as in catch a flight."

"Wait! What about coverage tonight? It's at The Bowl, for gosh sake. This is a paid working trip, remember, Genie?"

"I know. I know. But my mom left a message. I need to fly out and see my dad. He's in the hospital."

"Oh no. Is he okay?"

"Not sure. They're running tests on him."

"Well, okay, but can you fly out after the concert?"

"Jessie, I'm sorry, I have to get to my mom. I know she's probably in distress dealing with all the unknowns."

"Please, G! I mean, it's the freaking Hollywood Bowl for crying out loud! This is a big deal for his career. For my career, too. Please, this would mean a great deal to me. I need you to be there!"

"Okay, okay, but immediately following the concert, I'm heading to LAX."

This was an actual situation with my dad. But it happened a week ago. He was having indigestion pains that felt like a heart attack, he'd thought. He was fine and back home the next day after the test came back clear. I just wanted to get as far away from the Villa of Temptation as I could. I refuse to stay another night under the same roof as Pablo. The nerve of him trying to win me over with those beautiful long-stemmed orchids. It appears he was dead set on getting me in an uncompromising position. Those mesmerizing eyes and damn near-perfect physique would have any girl turning into a groupie. I had to remain professional and remove myself from the situation so he wouldn't have the opportunity to fraternize by being under the same roof overnight. I had spoken to him before, but the kid was relentless. I caught a glimpse of my reflection in the mirror. Who could blame him? I giggled to myself.

The day was wrapping up. Pablo surprised me today with his speech and interactions with the youth in East LA. He talked to them about how their family and community needed them to attend school and earn good grades, so they could attend any college they wanted. He encouraged them to read, write, express themselves, eat well, exercise, meditate, pray, and be their true selves. He reflected on how Nipsey Hussle gave back and uplifted his community by providing chances and opportunities to those who are often overlooked.

"Young men, I want each of you to go home today and tell your mothers, grandmothers, aunts, and sisters, 'thank you'. Black women are the most disrespected and overlooked beings on the face of this Earth. Listen to and respect every woman around you. You will go a long way with respecting others and yourselves."

He addressed the young girls about demanding respect for themselves. He encouraged them to love their uniqueness, to embrace and continually elevate their greatness. As we finished up by handing out free school supplies, gift cards, and lunches to the children, I saw Pablo inching toward me. He kept getting stopped by the parents thanking him, then the children wanted to audition their rapping skills, some adults,

                    THE DREAM LIFE

too. He was making a beeline for me when I heard Tony
shout his name. "Yo P! P! Over here, P!" I vanished before
he could find me again. I notified Jessie that I was heading to
Rodeo Drive to do some shopping before the show tonight.
She handed me a black card. "Here, charge it to this."
"Wait, we need to renegotiate my contract if there's a
lucrative expense account now involved? My fee is damn
near pro-bono."
"But you are being taken care of, right or wrong?" Jessie's
quick comeback changed the subject. I opened my mouth to
retort hastily, but decided to let her have this round. After all,
I did have a black card in my hand.
"Are you sure you want to give me this card? You know I
spare no expense when it comes to my shoe game." I said,
letting my guard down.
"No worries, Genie. Pablo's name is growing, and so are his
advances. Remember, this is a paid trip!"
"Alrighty then, if you say so." And just like that, I was on my
way.
The crew was back at the mansion by the time I returned
from shopping. My driver helped me unload the bags of shoes
and other unmentionables I had bought. Besides shopping in
Paris, Rodeo Drive was a place where I would often lose
track of time, going from store to store and upgrading my
already high-end wardrobe, much like Julia Roberts in *Pretty
Woman.* However, I would dare a sales associate to refuse
service to me, because that would be the last thing they'd dare
do. Working in this business, I received many sophisticated
wears for free. Fashion naturally became a part of my life

during childhood. Mommy-daughter dates often involved her dragging me into her office to buy merchandise for high-end department stores.

Her office would be piled high with the latest trends for us to try on. After hours of trying on label after label, we would vote on our favorites, and she'd make her decisions. Mom once told me that fashion isn't just what you wear, but a canvas for how you feel about yourself. She would preach that a woman walking in her divine femininity should never be without a good Rouge, quality perfume, great clothes, and heels. Even her bedroom slippers were heels. In those early years, I began to see fashion as a way to define looks that expressed my mood, culture, genre, and era. Every day felt like playing dress-up to me. Now, I see it as an expensive form of therapy I can wear.

"Where are you going with all those shoes?" Jessie asked me as I lugged the bags through the foyer of the suite. I walked over to her and handed her the Christian's she had been raving about two weeks ago that she couldn't find in Manhattan.

She jumped out of her skin before even opening the box. "Thank you! Thank you! Thank you!" She did her infamous happy dance and hugged me. "See, this is why you are better than diamonds, my friend!"

I shrugged my shoulders. "Don't thank me, thank the black card," I stated, handing it back to her. We got ready for our night at the Hollywood Bowl. Being the ultimate charmer that he is, Pablo booked massages, manicures, and pedicures for Jessie and me before the show. "This guy just doesn't know when to quit!" I shouted when the house manager delivered the specialists to our suite.

"Girl, why would you want him to quit?" Jessie said, sounding miffed.

"Ummm, remember, Will? As in William Dean Jones? My boyfriend, my lover, my heart?"

"Please," she threw her hands up. "Honey, who are you trying to convince, me or yourself?" I didn't reply.

"It's just work perks, geez, Genie. Stop acting like you don't like the attention."

"Attention can lead to other things. I don't want to go down that road again."

"Again? Are you talking about your sordid history with Boss?" My silence revealed the truth.

"Pablo is nothing like that money-hungry, misogynistic asshole, so relax."

Jessie couldn't stand Boss from the very beginning of my story with him. Their short and not-so-sweet story started when I introduced her to him as someone trying to make a few dollars for amateur night at his popular gentlemen's club in Harlem. Girls auditioned in droves for his team, but he only selected ten. They had the chance to walk away with $5,000 plus tips for the grand prize. Second place was $2,500, and third place was $1,000, plus they kept all tips earned during their dance. Jessie was a struggling college student trying to make ends meet on her own. I knew she needed the money, but she also had two left feet, so I asked Boss to make sure the votes were in her favor. He looked out for her and also tried to "advance" her career that same night. Jessie Grey, being Jessie Grey, went off on him. The strong-willed woman she is, she took it as an insult and said to him, "You just want to use me to fatten your pockets."

Boss's reply to her was, "Yep, just like that fat ass of yours." I scolded him for disrespecting her. He called her to apologize. It was a surprise, for sure, to find out through Boss Jessie was picking up a few shifts. When I asked her why she didn't tell me, she was brief, saying, "I guess job confidentiality isn't a thing anymore." She later confided in me that it was the most demeaning yet empowering feeling she had ever felt. It was always hard for her to let bygones be bygones. She would always give me flak for staying in contact with him. My connection to him was more profound than the money. It was about building generational wealth, or at least I thought so. This is a money-driven world. *Dinero* was the only language I needed to learn, according to him.

"Boss couldn't compare to Pablo even if he tried," Jessie continued.

"Listen to you. One measly encounter a decade ago, and you're still jaded."

She snatched her open robe shut and crossed her arms. "Oh no, I'm not the jaded one. But you're obviously the one still dick riding, Gennieee…" She would drag my name out like this when I got under her skin. "Does he still have a spell on you or what?" She was relentless.

"First of all, dick riding? Me? When have I ever? Secondly, it is I who cast spells, sweetie, not the other way around."

She rolled her eyes. "Weak! I don't want to hear it. He tried to solicit me, profit off me." I cut her off, throwing my hands up.

"J! Look at yourself! You're a bad bitch! What pimp would pass up an opportunity to pimp you?"

She began to laugh. I laughed, too. We sat in silence on the couch.

I wanted to ask the real reason for her disdain for Boss. In my heart, I knew it had to be more than her working at a job getting paid five times as much as she made in that one amateur night. I knew she had standards and morals about herself, but the cat was out of the bag now, literally.

The masseuse and nail technicians broke up the monotony as they arrived and began setting up the suite for relaxation. Dozens of candles, aromatherapy diffusers, and scattered roses adorned the room, and soft spa music was playing. I thought this setup was almost too romantic to share the moment with my best girlfriend, but it didn't bother me because my mind was on someone else. What harm could come from getting spa treatments? It's just work perks. After the long day at the youth center and shopping, my feet were sore.

Hate to admit it, but I was starting to appreciate the constant attention to detail Pablo was putting down.

CHAPTER 13

A dream coming untrue

Things had been in full swing at the LC company since Lauren had returned to Atlanta from her sabbatical. Everyone who walked through that door questioned amongst themselves where LC had disappeared for weeks without a call or trace, but no one would dare ask her. If they did, she'd tell them with a blunt face,

"Give me your nose so I can shove it up my ass since you wanna be in my shit." Lauren was as New York as the Yankees.

"Little Miss, I'm a freelancer who takes on low-paying jobs to spike my boss; you decided to come in today, I see," she said, pulling on a cig almost nearing the filter. I wave my hands to break up the smoke, coughing exaggeratedly. "Yuck. Blow your smoke in another direction. You really should think about quitting, LC."

"That ship has sailed, Rae, so do yourself a favor and let me die in peace," she said, putting the butt out on the bottom of her shoe.

"Who was the boy toy?" I asked, hoping not to get cursed at. She lowered her glasses, which already seemed to be at the tip of her nose. I stopped editing and caught her gaze. It felt as if she was saying something with her eyes. A deep stare that was worthy of a contest. "That good, huh?" I said, breaking the silent stare down. She shook out of the spell, saying, "You know, work hard, play harder." She moved closer, leaned in, and whispered loudly with breath that smelled of mint and cigarettes, "Listen, I need you to talk to the new shooter and the guy who was interning with him about not letting the bunnies encourage them to stay out late doing God knows what, and not missing a.m. shoots. Thanks."

"You mean let them go for lack of better judgment?"

"Would you, please? I'm too old and fragile to convince them of how impatient I am for that kind of unprofessional bullshit."

"Come on LC, you know how it is sometimes. We both had our share of street symphonies."

"Yeah, but the next day we had our asses on the set, nor did we sexually assault the models. Well, allegedly anyway."

"Say what now?"

"Quiet as kept, this is a claim that was brought to my attention. Did you hire the guy?

"What are you talking about, old lady? What guy?"

"The guy, Rae! The young shooters working the set yesterday for the Vogue shoot?"

"Oh, I have no idea. I wasn't there. But what happened?"

"Not sure about all the details. One of the models said that a photographer on the set yesterday was trying to stuff his third leg between her breasts at some strip club they visited. So, you know the drill."

"Okay, I'll find out who was on the set and speak with them about their conduct."

"Having my name attached to any kind of unsavory behavior like this will be my dream coming untrue. I won't have that, Rae! I'm too close to retirement for this shit! Give them the axe. Okay?"

"Sure, boss. Anything else?"

As she walked to the door, she turned back. Even though my attention was still on the screen, I felt her looking at me. I didn't take my eyes away from my work but asked her, "Anything else?"

LC said, "Rae." I took my eyes to meet her and waited for her to say what was on her mind. "Thank you."

"No worries," I said, and she walked out.

I told my assistant to gather the shooters that LC had instructed me to ditch. When they walked into my office, they were all smiles and raving about the bunnies in the middle of a swim shoot until I said, "Do you know why I have called you into my office?"

Miche stopped talking to Mark and said, "No, but I am sure we are about to find out why." He laughed and looked at Mark as if he wanted to receive a high five or something.

Mark's face told a story of guilt. He began, "Listen, Rae, I had car trouble if this is about being late to the morning shoot." I responded,

"Did you also have car trouble when hanging out the night before with the bunnies? Uhh, I meant the models from the shoot? They were on time. Why didn't you ask them for a lift? Let me ask you something, and your response will not determine your future employment at The LC company, but did one of you make an inappropriate advance towards…" I looked at the name my assistant jotted on the note. "The model… Jaslene?"

I looked at Mark. He squirmed in the chair and struggled with his words.

"I, I, I…"

Then Miche blurted out, "She was the one who pulled my dick outta my pants."

"Miche, shut up!" Mark said, punching him on the arm.

"Save it! Do you know what it means to work for The LC company?" I went on without pausing for them to respond to the rhetorical question. "You put integrity and professionalism on the line, not just for yourselves but for the woman who is the face of this company. Now, with that being said, your services are no longer needed. Thank you. That is all." Credibility is everything to LC. She always told me, "Never fuck with my time or money, or it's a wrap." The smiles they once had were now wiped from their smug faces. They sat there as if they hadn't heard me say 'that was all'. I walked over to open the door and motioned for them to leave with my hand.

Mark stopped and faced me as they exited my office. "Fuck you, Rae. You didn't even give me a chance to explain."

"You said enough. Good luck with your career in the future." One thing is for sure: they would need all the luck they could get after crossing Lauren Calloway.

I went into the area where they were shooting the swimsuit layout. Most of the thicker models were wearing one-pieces and cover-ups, looking extremely unflattering. The size twos were damn near naked. I walked over and said, "Alright, ladies, we're going to break for lunch and reshoot when you return. Be back in one hour." Toya, the first shooter on the set, approached me with such haste that I was surprised she didn't knock me over. "What the hell, Rae? You can't just come in and take over my shoot!" I put my arm around her shoulder and replied, "Now, Toya, we both know that's not true. But still, don't slash my tires. Just kidding, I don't drive. I appreciate the direction you were headed, but I have a different vision for this outcome. A more positive body imaging vision that you are going to love, I promise."

"So, I have to shoot this whole thing from the top? Perfect!" she grunted.

"Nope, I'm going to do it. You can hang around here and watch my vision come to life or leave early to make it to your daughter's ballet recital, your choice." I shrugged my shoulders and started to walk away.

Toya grabbed me, hugged me, planted a kiss on my cheek, then scooted out the door without thinking twice.

When the models returned from lunch, they were surprised to hear me instruct the wardrobe assistants to bring out the plus-size G-strings and bikinis. The entire shoot went

     THE DREAM LIFE

smoothly. Robin, one of the kindest models I have had the pleasure of working with over the years, approached me and said, "Rae, I can't believe you put me in that itsy bitsy teenie weenie bikini, and it's going to be in a magazine for my mama to see!"

I replied, "You worked it too, girl!"

She gave a shy yet shining smile, showing all her pearly whites. "I know I did! Thank you! It felt exhilarating to wear a bikini for a change, not the full-body bathing suit like in the 1950s."

After arriving at my place, a quarter after nine p.m., I decided to walk a couple of blocks down the street to this unique Ethiopian food truck that served some of the best fried injera Rangoon. During my little dinner stroll, light rain started to fall. The closer I got, the heavier the drops became. When I reached the usual spot where it was parked, it wasn't there. "Dammit, I walked all the way down here in the rain for nothing!" I took shelter from the raindrops under the bookstore's awning and quickly checked Instagram to see where they were posted tonight, only to find out they were permanently closed. "Fuck Atlanta?!!!" I yelled. It seems tough for small businesses to survive four seasons here, especially restaurants. I scrolled through Uber Eats on my phone for another quick food delivery.

As I trekked back to my place, I sensed someone behind me. I looked up from my phone and turned around. Before I could react, a figure dressed entirely in black appeared right in my face, with another ambushing me from behind. They forced me into a dark alley. "Give me everything you got?" the man shouted in my face.

My stomach sank. "Alright! Take my wallet! Take whatever!" Instead of reaching for my wallet, I carefully went into my tote for Peggy Sue, the little twenty-two my dad gave me when I left home for college. Before I could grab the concealed weapon, the attacker yanked the bag away and threw it to his co-conspirator. Without hesitation, he pulled out a .357 Magnum and struck me violently on the head with the grip. All I saw were dark orbits.

CHAPTER 14

"Don't wake me...I'm dreaming."

"God we know that you're strong and powerful, omnipotent, healing, and almighty God who made the oceans and seas. God, we ask that you open Gene Rae's eyes, heavenly father. Make her whole again. Just as you rescued Daniel and brought him safely out of the lion's den, please God, bring my child out of this coma...."

The voice sounded like my mother's. My instincts told me something was wrong because she was praying to God about "my child," and I was her only child. I still hear her persistent pleading with God to do the miracles described in the Bible.

I told my mind to tell my body to say, "I'm okay, Mom." But I couldn't move. I tried to open my eyes. As the light in the room filled my optic nerve, I felt a sudden rush to the front of my brain. I quickly closed my eyes. What had happened to me? Why couldn't I move? Why couldn't I speak to let her know *I was fine*? The only sign I could see was that I was in a hospital. During a quick glance, I saw Mom to my right on her knees, gripping the prayer beads her grandmother had given her, while Dad stood at the end of the bed, holding my feet. My dad started to pray. "We thank you, God, in advance for our daughter's healing. Thank you for being so merciful and gracious in keeping Gene Rae safe and alive. We thank you for sparing her life during her attack...."

Attack? I questioned myself internally. What attack? I wondered. I'm guessing something brutal had happened to land me in a coma.

I couldn't do anything but listen as my parents prayed for me nonstop. I mustered all the nerve I had to open my eyes again, but I just couldn't. I started to panic inside. I wanted to shout, scream, and cry, but none of those things happened. Just as I began to spiral in my thoughts, I heard my dad's voice. "I need to eat something other than hospital cafeteria food, and you need to eat something, period."

"James, I told you, I will fast and pray until my baby wakes up. Now please don't ask me again," my mom replied in a stern, quivering voice.

"Jenn, it's been days, honey. God is going to wake our baby up. You don't need to starve yourself; just have faith,"

     THE DREAM LIFE

my dad said. With his calming, reassuring words, he sounded as if he had convinced my mother that he had spoken to God himself and knew I would awaken from this deep sleep. She didn't budge. Silence filled the room. Moments later, I could hear my dad again.

"I have an idea. Since we both could use some fresh air and a brain clearing, how about we walk to Benihana and have your favorites, the spicy tuna and Las Vegas rolls?"

"James, you know I can't eat spicy foods anymore with my IBS, and as I said, I'm not eating or leaving until Gene Rae can eat or leave."

"But Jenn, Gene Rae is eating through the IV. You are the only one starving yourself."

"I'm not starving myself! I'm fasting," my mother replied, then started back praying and reciting scripture.

"Is not this the kind of fasting I have chosen to break the chains of wickedness, untie the cords of the yoke, set the oppressed free, and break every chain? Then your light will appear like the dawn, and your healing will come quickly. Your righteousness will go before you, and the Lord's glory will be your rear guard. The Lord will always lead you, satisfy you in a parched land, and strengthen your bones. You will be like a watered garden and a spring whose waters never run dry...."

My mother began to cry loudly and scream. "My baby, my baby! Lord, wake her, heal her, please, Lord!"

I suspected my dad was comforting her as her cries sounded muffled by his chest.

In my thoughts, I start to feel sad and angry. I want to know what's happening. I try to wake up, hold my mother, and tell her I love her beyond the galaxies. Then I almost experience an out-of-body sensation. For the second time in my life, I hear the bawling of the strongest, most fearless man I know. The only other time I remember him crying was when I left for college. And back then, it was just a few tears quietly streaming down his round cheeks. This time, my father's cries pull my soul outside of myself. I want to hug them both and tell them, "I'm fine. Stop crying and worrying." But even I don't know if that's true anymore.

CHAPTER 15

Broken Dreams

Once again, there was silence. I didn't know if it was the same day or if it had rolled over to the next. I didn't know anything —not even how many days had passed. I told myself to examine my body from the inside. I felt tubes in my nose, an IV in my arm, and a catheter in my bladder. I could feel my arms, hands, legs, and feet. I traced my senses back up to my head. Abruptly, I felt trauma. It felt as though my heart was beating heavily on my right temple. My intuition told me this injury was head-related.

My dad stated that days had passed, so I was knocked unconscious, but how?

"Jessie, child, you don't have to keep bringing new bouquets every time you visit. It's starting to look like a funeral home in here," I could hear my mom saying.

"I know, but Rae loves fresh flowers, and it makes me feel like I'm helping her somehow, even if she is not conscious."

Jessie! I thought. Even Jessie is here now. It made me feel even more perplexed and concerned about my health.

"Jessie, when does your flight leave?" my dad asked.

"I booked a late one, around 9 p.m. So, I will probably need to leave here by 6 p.m. I feel so guilty leaving her here like this. I wanted to extend my stay, but…."

"Child, it's in God's hands. We have to keep trusting and praying. God will show us a miracle in this obstacle. Just wait and see," my mom said. I could feel her rubbing my arm.

"I hope so," Jessie said.

"Aht- aht! No hope, so know so. Trust Him. If you have the faith of a mustard seed… remember me telling you girls that, when you were children?"

"Yes, ma'am, Mrs. Roman. I remember what you used to say to us," Jessie announced with a quiver in her voice.

Now, after hearing the upset in Jessie's voice, I knew this had to be serious. She hated coming to hospitals ever since she had to frequent them because her mom was in and out of them, witnessing her battling cancer at a young age.

She always told me, "Don't get sick because I won't be there at your bedside. But I will be there in spirit and send you some fresh orchids." Jessie's passionate disparagement of hospitals didn't hold up against this situation.

Moments of prayer, small talk, shared memories, and more prayers followed, then quiet passed.

Jessie broke the monotony.

"Do you all remember when you guys went on that coastal African cruise? I think it was the summer of ninth grade?"

"Don't remind her, Jessie. She was terribly seasick the entire time."

"Well, that summer, I broke that upstairs window, not Genie. You see, we were playing baseball, and you know I love hitting grand slams, and …" Jessie sounded as though she was trying to persuade a jury that I was innocent, and she was the guilty one.

My dad interrupted her. "See, Jenn. I told you Gene Rae didn't do it. You owe me a dollar." They all laughed.

"How did you know?" Jessie asked, her throat trembling. "Let's just say I know my daughter," replied my father. She's a great pitcher, but hitting outfielders was never her forte."

"That's if she would hit it at all." My parents shared another laugh.

"I'm so, so, so sorry, Mr. and Mrs. Roman. When G told me she would take the blame, I should have told her no. It was all my fault. I can reimburse you all right now. I'm sorry I let her take the blame. I shouldn't have…" Jessie went on, still riding her guilt trip into tears.

My dad interrupted her again. "Breathe. Jessie, calm yourself. Take a deep breath. Okay. Now, you feel better?" My dad's soothing voice calmed her. "It's okay, my dear. I know you're feeling overwhelmed with this matter, but trust me, being here in the flesh is repayment enough. I'm about to take a trip to the vending machine. Do you still enjoy a cold Pepsi?"

"Yes, yes, sir," Jessie replied, still caught up in her weeping.

"Okay, honey, you want anything?" he asked Mom. There was no response.

Before Jessie left, she whispered in my ear, "Mustard seeds are small just like me and you, but it's all the faith you need to make your prayers come true. I can't wait to see your beautiful brown eyes again, Genie. I miss you, girl," she kissed me on the cheek and bid farewell to my parents and then departed.

CHAPTER 16

In the wee hours of Thursday, November 26, Thanksgiving Day, my body became active. I listened to my parents as they debated about which one of my grandmothers made the best cornbread dressing.

"Now see, I know you have lost your mind. I'm finna get this nurse in here to check you out. Ain't no way that dry box bread yo mama would make could even be considered home cooking dressing." Seems as if my dad had fully adopted a Charleston drawl.

"James Russell Roman the third!" my mom shouted back. Any time his full name made it to the conversation, he knew to back off without hesitation. "Don't pay any mind to him, Will. If we were having our traditional Thanksgiving feast, he wouldn't be talking about my mama's dressing, just eating it!"

"I'm sure Nana's dressing was great, Mrs. Roman, God rest her soul, but Rae would also brag about how she loved yours the most."

"Well, where do you think I got the recipe from? My mama's homemade, from scratch, cornbread dressing! James is just being messy."

A blanket of silence fell over the room.

"Dad." My hoarse, shallow voice broke the silence.

"Gene Rae!" The excitement grew in my mother's voice as if she were trying to hit a Mariah Carey pitch.

"Nurse! Nurse! Honey, I'm going to get the nurse!" my dad said, exhilarated.

My eyes slowly opened and closed as they adjusted to the light. I could now see and hear my mother jumping up and down and praising God repeatedly for my awakening.

"My baby, my baby! Thank you, God! My baby has awakened! She's awake! This is the best Thanksgiving ever!"

A month had now passed since my coma caused by a physical assault. The swelling from the blunt force trauma to my head was so persistent that the doctors kept me heavily sedated to minimize brain activity, giving me time to heal. The blow also damaged my ability to remember events in my life. The doctor said I might regain my memory someday, or I might not. I didn't remember what had happened. They questioned me several times, but I couldn't recall anything from that day. Everything still felt so surreal. It was as if I were walking through a life unfamiliar to my own reality. My therapist suggested regression therapy to help find the person or people responsible. After reconnecting with Will, I learned he had been in close contact with one of his frat brothers, a detective with the Georgia Bureau of Investigation. The area where I was found had no working cameras, so the detectives on the case were having trouble locating the perpetrators. Will told me he wouldn't let the Atlanta Police Department rest until they found the offenders and prosecuted them to the fullest extent.

Will kept asking me questions like, "Do you remember the first time we kissed?" "What's the name of the pizza joint we'd meet at?" "Where was our first date?" and other random questions about our past. He believed that this would jog my memory and help me remember the incident. Although I mostly knew all those answers, I still had trouble recalling many precious moments I had once lived. I remember being a photographer. I remember growing up in Brooklyn. I knew I lived in Atlanta. I knew I could eat pizza for breakfast, lunch, and dinner without a second thought. James and Jennifer were my parents. Jessie has been my best friend since first grade. Will is my first true love. However, things were still fuzzy in my head.

I remember breaking my arm when I was younger, but I couldn't remember how it happened. Luckily, Jessie would remind me that it was because I slipped on a patch of ice while walking to school on a cold winter day in New York. She seemed to remember more about my life than I did when I had my full memory.

When I was finally allowed to go home, my parents stayed with me for a while until I convinced my mom that I could stay alert long enough not to fall asleep while cooking and that I was regaining some strength. I still felt hazy and drained, but my therapist emphasized that returning to my routine was essential for my healing. I knew I couldn't keep relying on my parents as a crutch. Still, I was petrified of the unknown. What if I forgot how to fly my filming drone during a wedding shoot, and it dropped and hit someone on the head? Deep down, I sensed that things felt off or unnatural. My mind kept saying, "You can do this, Rae." So, I just pushed myself to do small things—take a walk, cook something, go to the store. I told myself not to be afraid and to live my life one moment at a time. Yet, I felt like I was drifting through life on a passenger train that kept arriving at the same station every day with no way to change it. Every time my parents went to the market, they would purchase a month's supply of everything from my favorite foods to personal essentials.

Jessie became my roommate when my parents finally left. She claimed it was because Pablo had many events booked in the Southeast, so she wanted to be in a central location — Atlanta. I felt, though, that it was a plan devised by my mom. They rented a tour bus for travel to and from their gigs, so I mostly saw her during the weekdays when they were in Atlanta. I witnessed a new side of Jessie that I had never seen before. She became an excellent caregiver. She prepared my meals, did my laundry, arranged my schedule, and managed many tasks for me. Neither of us drove, so she would book

　　　　THE DREAM LIFE

Ubers for my doctor's appointments and therapy sessions, and she would accompany me whenever she was available. One day, she even rescheduled her meeting to take me to Neiman's because I needed a little retail therapy, she said. Pablo's management temporarily hired another photographer I arranged through the LC company to take on my previous assignments. He would continually send words through Jessie to encourage my healing. His innate charm was coded in messages she relayed. One day, she arrived with white, long-stemmed orchids and a note. It read,

"THE WEATHERING OF LIFE CAN SOMETIMES CHANGE THE FEATURES OF A MOUNTAIN. MOUNTAINS MAY ERODE, MOUNTAINS MAY BLOW THEIR TOPS, AND THEY CAN ALSO BE PRONE TO AVALANCHES. BUT IN ALL ITS TRAVESTIES, IT WILL STILL BE A MOUNTAIN. MAJESTIC AND STRONG, IT WILL REMAIN. NO ONE CAN CHANGE THAT. YOU ARE A STRONG, FORMIDABLE MOUNTAIN. THINK OF EVEREST WHEN YOU'RE FEELING DOWN OR LOST AND KEEP CLIMBING. NO WEAPON THAT IS FORMED AGAINST YOU SHALL PROSPER. PRAYING FOR YOU, RAE."

I told no one, even though I knew Jessie saw it. I posted this note on the mirror in my bathroom. The words helped me get through the day. When my thoughts turned negative, I would redirect them to two words, 'think Everest'. 'Think Everest' became my new way of seeing the world. When I finished long days on shoots, I would think of Everest. I wanted to personally thank him for those words and share how they gave me a new perspective on life.

I sent word through Jessie to inform Pablo that I wanted to see him. She gave me the side-eye when I told her. "Hmmm. Guess his influence was strong enough not to forget, huh?"

"Honestly, if there was something to forget about him, I probably never knew it to begin with."

"Okay, if that's what you want, I will be sure to let him know. I'm sure he'll be delighted. When?"

"Soon. Before I fly out to Cali next weekend."

Jessie's expression changed swiftly. "Traveling? Already?"

"How long am I supposed to live with the memory of this assault shadowing my life? I have to move on with my life, J."

"Are you sure you are ready?" she questioned me as if she were Jennifer Roman herself.

"Girl, I'm Everest. No weapon formed against me shall prosper. I'll be fine."

"Okay, Everest. Since you are going out that way, I guess I'll tag along for Pablo's show at Mint."

"Really, Mom! Does he even have a show?"

"G, what? I'm serious. We just booked it this morning. I forgot to tell you. And yes, really. You need to appreciate my overbearing motherly instinct. Just looking out for you, girl, don't trip."

"I appreciate all you have been doing for me lately, but I'm okay! It's time for me to put my big girl drawers on again and keep climbing."

"Okay, but I'm still going. Not because of you, because it's my job, so deal."

Geez, you would have thought she was the older one.

    THE DREAM LIFE

CHAPTER 17

Daydreamer

The trip to LA drained me more than I expected. Jessie and I shared a rental instead of her staying at Pablo's pad with his crew. I arrived a day early at the photo shoot location. It was for visuals of a new eco-friendly foreign car making waves in the U.S. The shoot was near the cliffside by the Griffith Observatory. I don't know if it was the height or the smog, but I started feeling dizzy while adjusting my angles. My second shooter, Jim, followed my instructions to call Jessie just in case something happened. I could hear the panic in his voice.

"Is, is this Jessie? Help, please! Rae, Rae, she is ummm, ummm. She asked me to call you. Rae, what do you want me to say? I need to call 911, Rae."

I cut him off, snatching the phone from his tight grasp.

"J. Come to the address I texted you I'd be at today." It was all I could muster in a fading voice. When I regained consciousness, I was lying in a hospital bed at the ER. The doctor explained that my scan didn't reveal anything abnormal. He instructed me to take a few days off and schedule an appointment with my primary doctor upon my return to Atlanta. He also suggested that I don't fly for the time being.

After telling me I shouldn't work or fly, I tuned out everything he mentioned. There was money to be made and a mountain to climb. I had the opportunity to open my eyes again and come out of a coma. I wasn't cheery about being told to stay put. It was my time to make my name bigger and expand my brand. I couldn't live my life with my attack shadowing me forever. If I ever hoped to advance my career, there was no time to waste, which that unfortunate event taught me. So, I did what any ambitious-hearted person would do. I did my job. Everything went excellently, too. I never really appreciated Jim's work before, but he was extra supportive, doing the entire shoot that day. I let him take the lead, and he demonstrated such eagerness and perfection with every snap he captured. Jessie even came to lend a hand, although I knew it was to catch me if I fell.

When we returned to the hotel, long-stemmed orchids had been placed around the entire suite. From whom, you might ask? The one and only Pablo tha Picasso. He was giving Will

   T H E   D R E A M   L I F E

some competition. I must admit, the chase was flattering, especially since the man I had loved since I was a preteen seemed to have fallen off the Earth. The first few weeks after I was discharged from rehab, Will wouldn't leave my side. He seemed more concerned about finding whoever did this to me rather than about my well-being. Now, months later, he was back knee-deep in the many responsibilities that accompany a six-figure income.

Jessie went over and opened the note in the arrangement. "Damn, Pablo is jonesing for you, G!" she exclaimed.

"You think?" I replied sarcastically.

"I've wanted to thank him face-to-face for all the love and his encouraging words. They helped me come to grips with my will to live my life more fully than ever before."

"Well, you know he is here in LA. I can call him over if you want." She waited quietly for my response.

"Yeah. Do that."

"Oh shit, Will ass better watch his neck because someone is coming for it," she giggled.

"No one, I mean no one. Could ever take Will's place in my heart," I reminded her.

"Maybe not his place in your heart, but certainly his place in those lonely sheets," she remarked, continuing to find hilarity in the situation.

"Whatever, Miss Messy. I'm taking a shower to wash this day off me."

"Yeah, go ahead and get cleaned up for your boo, girl."

I closed the door to my bathroom to drown out her laughter.

I was sitting in the shower, wondering what this distant feeling was that had suddenly overtaken my and Will's relationship. We had always been a couple that understood each other's career goals, and that the amount of traveling our careers required would often put us miles apart. However, this close call with the Grim Reaper had me reconsidering many things I thought were inevitable. Did I want to remain this distant from my lover? Are Will and I growing apart because of all the distance created by our schedules? Life would be so strange if we decided to go our separate ways. I know for a fact that familiarity brought us this far. When we broke up during our sophomore year of college, it was because neither of us could endure the distance. At the time, I just knew that that was the end of us. It was my first heartbreak because I felt Will was the guy for me. Ultimately, though, it was best for us to finish our college years single.

Jessie interrupted my deep thought with a knock at the bathroom door.

"Yes, J?"

"Pablo says he'll be here in ten."

Ten! Getting anywhere in LA took at least 30 to 40 minutes. "OKAY. Thanks, J." I thought, damn, if I could only get my real man to come running that fast.

I finished washing the day away and slipped into my yellow cotton maxi lounge dress. Moments later, I stepped out of my bedroom. Jessie was standing outside my door. "He's at the door. Buzz him in?"

"How did he get here so quickly?"

     THE DREAM LIFE

"Well, he said ten minutes. It's been twenty. P deadass sprung." She laughed, then rubbed her stomach. "Damn. I got the munchies all of a sudden."

I walked over to buzz him in.

"You feel like Chinese tonight?" I asked her.

"You read my mind. Hu's Szechwan?"

"Yep, that's cool."

Pablo was coincidentally wearing a yellow Gucci tracksuit with some crisp white Air Force ones. He was wearing his favorite Cuban link necklace, which he often wore. I must admit, he was always dressed well and smelled so damn good. Before dismissing herself, Jessie asked, "What do you want from Hu's? I'm going to put in the order now."

"Same thing. Mandarin chicken salad and egg rolls. Pablo, we're ordering dinner from Hu's. You want anything?" I asked him.

"Oh, is this a dinner invite?" he sounded surprised.

"If that's what you want to call it, we don't have to obscure it with titles, though," I replied.

"Finally," he said, with his hands pressed together in a prayer position and looking upward. "I wouldn't pass up the chance to dine with you, Ms. Roman." He eyed me with that sly look, as if I were the meal.

Pablo decided to order a bit of everything from the menu. Jessie picked off my plate as usual and ate hers, too.

I had been pulled away for an emergency conference call to discuss the itinerary for an upcoming business trip to London. I wasn't sure if I was ready for it, but I felt like I needed to dive back into my ordinary life as a photographer with wings.

"Ask Jessie to accompany you as your assistant. At least that way you will have someone who knows London and you like the back of their hand. Bye," LC blurted out, then quickly hung up the phone.

I didn't think about asking Jessie because she was bent over enough, letting me use her as a crutch. I went back to the dining area, where the two of them were laughing so hard they were gasping for air.

"Did I miss the punchline?" I interrupted.

"G, remember when you found that spider in your shoe, and you were so terrified to wear closed shoes that you wore flip-flops for months."

"I hope it was summertime," Pablo questioned.

"Hell no, it was the dead of winter in Brooklyn," Jessie disclosed. "We were walking to school one morning and she busted her ass so bad on some black ice. You had to be there. She was practically airborne. But her arm broke the fall, which, not coincidentally, also broke her arm. All because she refused to put her feet into closed shoes." She was laughing until real tears began to fall.

"Well, I don't remember it being as funny as when you fell from the top of the auditorium bleachers at the Christmas Pageant that time."

She cut her chuckling immediately and put on a 'now why did I have to bring that up' face.

"Nah, don't get all serious now. The funniest part was how quiet the crowd was. It was as if they knew you were about to take a tumble. You trembled in those damn six-inch heels so badly. Then boom! You hit every step like a brick."

Pablo tried to shift the dark humor. "Okay, moving on from embarrassing stories."

"Aht-aht, P, hold up. Genie, if only Ma Dukes had taught me to walk in Stilettos like yours did at the tender age of two years old, then maybe…" She said with a sharp tone.

"Is that supposed to be a comeback or an insult? Cause it didn't do what you thought it would." Jessie and I continued to laugh and share many hilarious memories with Pablo.

She passed the torture torch to Pablo. "Okay, P, tell us something embarrassing about yourself so we can complete this circle of trust."

Pablo indulged us and began to share his most embarrassing stories from his memory bank. He even recounted that he was a bit of a nerd who would get bullied because he was a superlative amongst his peers in school.

Jessie interrupted his walk down childhood trauma lane. "Why is it that we bully and make fun of the nerds as a society? They're the ones that most bullies have to end up working for in the long run."

The room fell quiet. Jessie dismissed herself from our company. "I miss having you around at my shows and taking pics and videos of us. Life on the road is just not the same without you there. Lately, I've been yearning for a sense of normalcy. I'm realizing that your truth and presence kept me grounded and focused on long-term goals."

I didn't know how to respond, so I didn't.

Then I uttered, "I thought you loved that rockstar glitz and fame lifestyle. Tired of it so soon?"

"Well, Rae, as they say, all that glitters ain't gold."

I responded, "So, you're not feeling the music industry anymore? It happens when real people get a taste of how phony it truly is."

"I just wanted to inspire others and build a lasting legacy. Honestly, music was just a way to keep my ass out of trouble. Even though I was considered the nerdy, smart boy, it didn't save me from finding trouble. Peer pressure was a mutha growing up in LA," he said, sighing, then changed the subject. "But as long as you're well and healing, that's all I care about. So, how long have you lived in Atlanta?" he asked while he started picking at the remaining scraps on his plate.

Here we go with the small talk. Something that I couldn't stand. There is so much big talk to be had in the world. Why waste it with trivial jargon?

"Listen, Pablo, I wanted to thank you for your good wishes and support personally. Your note gave me that oomph I needed to get back on the horse. I keep those words right here." I said, pointing to my head.

"I'm glad I could support your recovery, Rae. Just recalling that night makes my anger resurface repeatedly. I believe you see that, and I know you have a boyfriend," he said, with air quotes, "but I'm craving you. I was drawn to you before I even met you. To me, this feels like destiny fulfilling itself." I listened but said nothing. Honestly, his words helped me heal, reminded me of who I am. His intense focus on me made me realize that love without obsession can sometimes feel dully.

As midnight approached, our conversations became more in-depth. It was probably because Jessie had come back into the mix and was pouring us Saké bombs. Pablo recounted his childhood struggles growing up with a single mother after his father's unexpected death from a heart attack. Soon, the discussion and drinks transitioned to playing 'never have I ever' with Hennessy VSOP. The next thing I knew, Jessie was in the bathroom, revisiting her dinner.

I turned to Pablo, who didn't seem phased by any of it. "Are you not feeling all these shots?"

"Ummm, yeah, but I'm feeling you a bit more," his slick tongue responded.

"Lemme walk you out. Text me when you get to wherever you're staying, so I know you made it safely." I stumbled, and he caught my arm before I completely hit the floor, embarrassing myself.

"Whoa, Rae. Let me walk you to your bed instead, so I know you made it safely." He was smoother than butter with his delivery. As he pulled me back up to my feet, my shaky legs softened into the curve of his arm. He stood at the door, holding me a little longer than necessary. Then he kissed me.

Chapter 18

Like a dream

Maybe it was instant regret that plunged into my stomach or the mixture of alcoholic beverages as I lunged from his grasp, almost not making it to the toilet in time. Once I composed myself, I called Will since I couldn't reach him earlier. It was 5:15 a.m. here and 8:15 a.m. in New York. He was scheduled to finalize a business deal all weekend and return to Atlanta on Tuesday, just in time for us to drive to Charleston on Wednesday for another attempt at Thanksgiving dinner with my parents on Thursday. After last year's travesty of us all spending Thanksgiving in the hospital, he was more than happy to spend it celebrating great health and wealth, or so he said.

The phone kept ringing. I sank back, still clutching it. Just As I began to drift off into Dreamland, I felt my phone vibrate. in my hand. It was him. I quickly sat up, feeling nausea creeping over me once again.

"Hey, beautiful, sorry, I missed your call."

"Hold on for a sec." I had to hurl again.

When I returned to the phone, he said, "Sounds like somebody had a turnt up night. What did you get into?"

"Not much, just dinner and Saké bombs with friends. Are we still on for Thanksgiving?"

"Rae, for the hundredth time, yes!" he replied, sounding annoyed with me.

"Damn, what a way to respond."

"I apologize. I'm a little frustrated with this deal. Everything seems to be falling apart," he ranted.

"Do you want to talk about it, love?"

"Nah, I know it's too early there, and hearing you vomit in the background, I can tell you need some rest. Just know I love you, and I can't wait to spend my very first Thanksgiving with you. Things were different this time last year. I am grateful you are alive and doing well, my love."

"Wow, I never thought I'd hear those words come out of your mouth. Thanks, babe. I am grateful, too!"

"Yeah, I can't believe it either, but it's time to try something new. Carpe diem, right?"

After hanging up with Will, I realized that I had been straddling the fence with my feelings lately. Even though I told myself I wasn't into Pablo, I was. Perhaps it was his constant presence or his outright confessions of attraction to me. I knew what I needed to do.

Needless to say, I woke up with a hangover from hell. When I finally crawled out of bed, it was almost 2 p.m. I went into the kitchen to concoct my infamous hangover remedy. Jessie was already there mixing the ingredients.

"Hey, G. You feel like shit, too?" I just nodded yes without speaking.

"How late did Pablo stay?" she asked.

"Not too late. He left right after he kissed me."

Her eyes bulged from their sockets.

"He kissed you?!"

I fell silent after I blurted out that bit of information. It was honestly word vomit. But now that I had revealed it, I couldn't undo it. Her astonishment made me feel guilty even though I wasn't the one who initiated the kiss.

"Ugh, Genie?" She wouldn't fold.

"What?" I responded nonchalantly.

"What? I want to hear details - now!" Jessie demanded.

"It was nothing, just a harmless kiss." At this point, I was halfway in the fridge, reaching for nothing really, just not wanting to expose the guilt on my face.

"Genie, come on out of the refrigerator and give me the juicy details, girl. I have your hangover drink right here. I know you're not about to cook or eat anything."

I slowly brought my frozen body out and looked at her, "Whaaaaat?! He kissed me! Big deal!"

"Ooohweee! Look at you, little miss thrill seeker creeper."

"You know what, I'm too hungover to process this." We sat at opposite ends of the dining table, sipping our remedy tea. "Do you think I should tell?" I asked her.

"Tell who?" she inquired.

"You know who."

"Will?"

"No, Jessie, the priest... Who else? Yes, Will!"

She looked out the window, then stood up with her mug and walked over to the window. "I hear it's supposed to be a frigid winter this season. They are suggesting people who travel in and out of the northeast for work may have to live there due to the blizzards predicted in the forecast."

I stared at her, feeling nauseous, waiting for her to arrive at a point. She said nothing, just stared out the window. "Where are you getting this meteorologist insight from? And what does that have to do with telling Will?"

"Exactly, G! One thing has absolutely nothing to do with the other." My face was all twisted looking at her.

"Are you still drunk, J?"

"Listen, girl. What do you think he'll do about it if he knows about the blizzards predicted to come to New York this winter?"

"Buy a bigger jacket? Stock the pantry? I'm stuck on where you're taking this, J."

"Right, he'd be ready and plan for the blizzard only because he's been enlightened. But if he wakes up in the middle of the night to a blizzard he had no idea about, there's nothing he can do about it."

"Okay, I'm going to say this slowly.... huuuh?"

"Genie, how are you not understanding this?"

"J, you know you get super philosophical when you are tipsy. Just answer me straight. Should I tell Will about the kiss, yes or no?"

"I'm not trying to get in y'all's messy relationship, but no. He can do nothing about an unexpected blizzard now that the snow is already on the ground." She picked up my empty mug and walked into the kitchen to put both hers and mine in the dishwasher. She returned and sat near me, this time with a jovial look on her face. "Now, how was it?"

"Listen, I'm only sharing this with you and no one else. OKAY?"

"Who am I going to tell, G?

"You better not tell a soul." I paused, closed my eyes, and relived his soft lips falling on mine. They were supple and sweet. I slowly inhaled and exhaled.

"Damn, girl. It must be a bigger deal than you previously thought if you gotta do all that."

"You know what the funny thing is, it was just like a dream I had of him kissing me once before."

"Genie, you're always dreaming stuff that happens in real life. I wish I could be clairvoyant like you."

"At first, I thought he was coming closer to give me a goodnight hug, but he instead gave me a juicy smack right on the lips. Even in my dreams, I didn't feel this airy. I think I'm developing an attraction to him, J." Her eyes widened as I confessed.

"Well, we know one thing for sure: he's been attracted to you since before y'all even met. So at least you're not alone in your feelings."

    THE DREAM LIFE

"You know how I am, J. I can't hide the truth from Will."

"G, is there really anything to tell? No! He kissed you! Big deal, and who knows what Will got going on while he's always MIA."

The look I gave her was deadly. "What's that supposed to mean?"

"G, you know I love you to infinity, but…" she paused.

"But what?" I walked into the kitchen, waiting for her to explain the dread that I never wanted to acknowledge.

"Never mind. Do what you feel is best for your relationship. I have promo runs and meetings to set up, so let me get my day started."

"Avoidance. Classic Jessie Grey!" I yelled as she ignored me and walked into the bedroom. She didn't even look back.

I must admit that 'but' lingered over my head like a halo.

I was no angel in the past, and neither was Will, but I wanted our relationship to be infidelity-free this time. No, I didn't kiss Pablo back, but I would be lying to myself if I didn't say that his presence and that kiss made me yearn for more.

CHAPTER 19

Dreamcatcher

R ae, I have someone named Jessie Grey on the line for you. He said it's urgent," my new receptionist, Olivia, paged in, interrupting my final thought at the end of the staff's morning meet-ups at the LC company. She completely ignored my strict policy of holding all calls and messages until after our meetings. I'm guessing the emergency verbiage made her disregard my direct order— no interruptions unless urgent.

"I'm sorry about that interruption, everyone. Now, if we want to... to... wait, what was I talking about? Ah, now I lost my thought." Lizzie blurted,

"You were talking about how we could mimic a Spike Lee film for this activist shoot."

"Right, Lizzie. Thanks for being my brain on paper." I gave her two thumbs up.

"Okay, so you all think about which Spike Lee film would speak to this spread. Mine would be *Do the Right Thing*, simply because it reflects the same police injustices and brutality that are sadly still current today. TK, you and Brandi take care of the fine details, including approvals, clearances, and all the red tape. Melissa and Rod, you guys get the wardrobe worked out. Melissa, you can contact Holli, the VP at Swatches and Sew, for some samples. She owes me a favor."

"Sure thing, boss."

"Does anybody have anything else?... No? Okay, let's get to work, people."

As I gathered my things, I noticed Francisco walking toward me instead of exiting.

"Rae, what's been up with LC?" he asked, concerned.

"What do you mean?" I stopped what I was doing and gave him my undivided attention. I'm not one for office gossip, so I knew it was serious if he was inquiring about the happenings of my most trusted mentor.

"Listen, I know you're not one to gossip, and I wasn't even going to bother you because you are still going through your healing and everything, but she's been MIA for weeks. You know how obsessed she can be with this place sometimes, so it seems strange to me that she's been ghost."

"Interesting, but I'm sure her absence has a reason. One that she would have shared if she wanted us to know." He walked out with an attitude that screamed, "Thanks for nothing, heifer." Lauren and I had been thick as thieves ever since we met years ago when I waitressed at the Sundial restaurant in downtown Atlanta. If there was something to call attention to, I am sure she'd be the first to inform me.

Sitting at my desk, I couldn't dismiss Francisco's concerning tone from my head. I had been so wrapped up in my health concerns and matters of the heart that I hadn't paid much attention to work lately. Honestly, I was still trying to adjust to my new perspective and conjure up the old me, who was revered as a formidable mountain.

I paged Olivia to come to my office. My bubbly receptionist tried to make a good impression during her first week by pleasing many of the staff—bringing in bagels, treating the other receptionists to her homemade candles, and being overly eager to lend a helping hand instead of finishing the task I had assigned her. However, she was brown-nosing the wrong people—or, should I say, the wrong person—at the agency. She came in skipping like a schoolgirl. "I must give her the rundown before this gets out of hand," I said to myself.

"Oh, excuse me, Ms. Roman. Are you talking to someone? Is now good?"

"Hey, Olivia. Have a seat." She sat on the arm of the chair. "I'll make this quick because I know you have many tasks to complete. Do you remember when I discussed that there should be absolutely no interruptions during meetings because of how critical interruptions could be to our creative ideas?"

"Yes, but the guy said it was an emergency."

"Okay, first, Jessie is a girl. And I'm your boss. Understand?" I waited for any indication that she comprehended what I was saying, but she just sat there staring.

"Is that a yes or a no?" I questioned again.

"Oh yes, I'm sorry, sometimes I often go into involuntary daydreams, but yes, boss, I hear you loud and clear. I apologize for the interruption this morning. It won't happen again." She stood up to walk out, and then she turned back. "But what if it is an important emergency, like for real, for real?"

"Tell you what, if it's not someone with the likes of Michelle Obama trying to get me on the line, it can wait. Scratch that. If it's not Michelle or my mama, don't even bother. Okay?"

"Got it, boss."

"Thank you! And get Lauren on the phone for me, please."

"Will do, right away."

Moments later, she yelled from the door, "Her phone keeps going to voicemail, Rae."

While I was finishing responding to work emails, I saw Jonathan glide by my door. "Hey, Jon Jon!" I shouted out to him.

"First of all, hi. Second, no one but my mother still calls me Jon Jon. This must be important. What's the favor?"

"Aht-Aht, don't do that…you know we go way back. By the way, how is Ms. Val doing?"

He sat down and started to pour out unsolicited family issues to me.

"Dang boo, sorry to hear about all the dilemmas. Why didn't you come to talk to me sooner?"

"Girl, please, you have enough on your brain than hearing about my daily life drama."

"My door is always open for you, my friend."

"Thanks, girl. Let me get back to styling and profiling this upcoming wardrobe."

"Alright, boo. Thanks for catching me up."

As he walked out of my office, he quickly returned to ask, "Oh yeah, what was it you needed when you called me in here?" I rolled my eyes back, searching for the answer.

"Oh, I remember now. Sorry, my mind is really cloudy these days. I wanted to know the last time you talked to or saw LC?"

"Ooooo. It's been a hot minute. I thought you two were thick as thieves and talked every day. What's going on?"

"Nothing's going on. Francisco just informed me that she's been out of the office a lot lately. I've also been out of the office so much since the incident, and I'm working on other projects. I'm just trying to catch back up on my life."

"So, you haven't seen or talked with her either?"

"I talked to her on the phone, but now, looking back, that was over a week ago. You know this place is her real home, so her not being accounted for more than a week unless it's business-related is unusual."

"Yeah, it is weird not having the smell of cigarettes stink up the place."

We laughed, and his Daddy-long-legs went strutting out the door.

"Oh, Jon Jon! Jon Jon!"

     THE DREAM LIFE

"Oh, so I wasn't clear, hun? Nix the nickname."

"Let's not get snappy, honey. I just wanted to know what hospital your mom is having surgery in, so that I can send her some get-well-soon flowers?"

"Aww, Rae, you are such a sweetie pie. She'll be at Piedmont."

"Okay. Make sure you take some days off if you need to go help her or just be there since your brother is MIA."

"If he knows what's best for him, he'll stay MIA 'cause if I see him, he'll be DOA. Stealing from my mama like he ain't got no damn sense. How do you steal from someone who gave you life? Just trifling."

"I know, but we need to try to find him treatment, not just throw him to the streets. That's if he does show up at the hospital."

"Rae, honey, there are certain times that you have to wash your hands with people completely, even if they're your family."

Two days later, LC was still ghost. I decided to take advantage of the driver Will had arranged for me and asked him to take me out to LC's house before heading home from work. Before I got out of the car, I called again, but there was no answer. I'm not one for popping up on people, but I couldn't let another day go by without seeing or speaking to her.

I rang the doorbell several times. I knew she didn't have an alarm system, just fake cameras and signs. Luckily, I knew where she kept the spare key. When I opened the door, I shouted her name as loud as possible to alert her to my presence. She was a notorious gun collector, so I didn't want this visit to end badly for me. The house was drafty and dark, with a stale, smoky smell. Her office still had the dreamcatcher I had hung years ago, because she used that space more than anywhere else in the house. She fussed at me, saying, "I don't need anything catching my dreams. Good and bad. That's what life is all about." It was also empty—no layouts, photos, or memos were scattered about like usual. The bedrooms, great room, and bathrooms were all clear.

I got on the intercom. "LC, it's Rae. Where the hell are you in this huge mansion?" I waited for minutes at the intercom, but there was no reply as I continued to search the halls of her estate. I was relieved to see someone finally. It was Connie. Her longtime caregiver turned housekeeper looked to be wearing large headphones from the '80s. "Oh, thank God! Connie!" I yelled over the second-floor staircase banister. She didn't have a clue that I was there, let alone shouting her name. I could hear the music echoing from her headphones, filling the house's emptiness. I started running back down to the second floor to catch up with her. She was moving as if she were speed walking.

When I did finally come up behind her, I almost startled the life out of little Ms. Connie. "¡Ay Dios mío! Ms. Rae! You scared me to death. What are you doing, trying to scare me out of my skin?"

"I am so sorry, Ms. Connie. Where's LC?" I said, panting and trying to catch my breath from the chase.

She stopped her Walkman and said in broken English, "Ms. Calloway? She no here."

"Well, where is she?" I said, starting to worry.

"She tell me she won't come back until she makes peace with her father." Connie started her music again and walked off.

"Wait, what do you mean? Is she okay? Where is she?" I was starting to feel light-headed.

"I gotta sit down. Can I have some water, please?" Connie came back minutes later holding a tall glass of her famous red Kool-Aid. Infamous diabetes in a cup that would keep LC and me up on late hours in her home office, envisioning ideas and working on countless layouts. "Thanks, Connie."

"Are you okay, Ms. Rae? I hear about your troubles. Ms. Calloway was so worried about you." Her face showed much concern.

"Thanks, Connie. I'm just taking it day by day. So, did LC say where she would be? She hasn't been to work in days. She's not answering calls or responding to messages. This is not like her." I was hoping Connie would put my jangled nerves to rest, but all the information she had was that LC was going to make things right with her father.

CHAPTER 20

Back down dream lane

When I arrived at my condo, I saw this guy with a familiar demeanor and stance at the desk, talking to the concierge. I couldn't believe my eyes. It was Boss! What the hell was he doing here? I stood there for a minute, perplexed, then walked over to the desk.

"Well, look what the cat drug in?"

He turned around. His expression lit up. "Boogie-Down!" He hugged me, scooped me off my feet, then began spinning in circles. "Whoa! Whoa! Down, chief! You know I have vertigo." He put me down.

"Sorry. Just happy to see you are here in the flesh...alive!" Apparently, he got the news about the assault.

"Oh, okay. So, the news about the attack finally reached you. Come on." I walked off and headed to the elevator.

When I got to my place, I prepared both of us drinks—Henny V.S.O.P. with a wedge of lemon for Boss. I poured myself a Basil Hayden double with an orange twist. We went out on the terrace so he could puff on his Cohiba. The fall weather felt nice and crisp. The heater, fire pit, and drink had me feeling nice and warm. I brought him up to date on all the drama occurring. He told me he'd fallen in love with a Cuban woman and had lived in Havana with her for months. He even hinted that she wanted him to bring her to the States and tie the knot.

"Sounds a lil' green card-ish, if you ask me, but if you like it, I love it," I said, collecting our now-empty glasses. "Would you like a refill?"

Boss said, "Do you even have to ask, Shorty?"

"Actually, come inside. I'm going to order takeout."

"Bet! I'm dead ass starving too. Chinese? Hsu's?" he said, with hope in his voice.

"Well, I had a taste for Thai, but you're the guest, so why not?" He rubbed his hands together and made that grin people have when they're hungry and offered a free meal.

"So, how come you didn't reach out earlier?" I was curious but didn't care either way.

"Hello, I told you I was in la-la lover's land with my Cubana honey. When I got back to New York, Tiny Tim told me what happened..."

"Tiny Tim? You still mess with him after..." I interrupted.

He threw his hand up. "Nah, I don't really fuck with Tim because he is with that scamming shit too much, but I ran into Shorty around the way, and he told me what happened to you…"

"How the fuck… did Tiny Tim know about my incident?" I scratched my head. "You know what, never mind. Never mind," I said.

"Man, Boogie, I was fucked up in the head, too, after hearing about it. I wanted to come to your rescue immediately, but my phone and Mac were inside my satchel, which I had mistakenly left in the cab that took me to the airport. I lost all my contacts and info…."

"Wait, you didn't have your Apple ID or have your info backed up in the Cloud?" I interjected.

"Boog, no offense to y'all 'iPeople' and the Apple products, but I don't fuck with all that cloud shit. Too many Feds are watching and listening, but anyway, I didn't have any way to get in touch with you when I found out. I thought about going to your old girl's mom's house, but nah, I didn't need any conflict. I decided to hop on a plane and come down south to check on you myself, na mean?"

"Who's the old girl? Also, they are watching with or without your permission. Regardless of a damn phone." I protested.

"Jessie's mom. She still on Ocean Ave.?" he asked.

"Nah, she moved back to the UK years ago," I replied.

"Oh," he shrugged.

How would that have been conflicting if he had contacted me through Mrs. Grey, I wondered?

   THE DREAM LIFE

"What do you mean you didn't want any conflict?" I wondered no longer.

"Now, Boog, you know she's had a stick up her ass about me ever since she used to dance at that joint I had in Harlem."

"Why?" Just as I was about to probe, Jessie came walking upstairs. She stood there looking like a deer caught in headlights.

"Hey, J. Look who came to visit." She made an about-face turn and headed back down into my guest suite, which she had been occupying for weeks now. The door slammed as confirmation.

"See what I mean now? Conflict—don't need it, and don't go looking for it. Your darkroom got any shots of beautiful women in lingerie?" He swiftly changed the subject, rubbing his palms together. What about your Cubana wanna-be wifey?" I reminded him.

"Hey, a man's gonna be a man, B." He retorted with a slimy grin.

"I haven't been developing any photos lately. I've been leaving that for the team at work," I revealed to him.

"But isn't that like therapy for you? Taking raw photos and watching the darkness bring them to light, or whatever that shit you would tell me when I told you to get them developed at CVS photo lab to save time."

I chuckled at him, trying to recall things I didn't think he was even hearing back in the day.

"Nah, but for real, Ma. Maybe that's the therapy you need for healing that big ass head of yours."

The buzzer went off. "That's the food." I got up to answer the door. Boss excused himself to the bathroom to wash up.

I put the food on the table and went downstairs to check on Jessie. "What's up, J? How was your day?" I asked, but no response. Then she finally spoke.

"What the hell is he doing here?" she asked, giving me a stern look.

"Okay, what is it with you two? I want to know right now, today." She sat there quietly like a mouse. "Well, we're about to eat. I ordered the duck for you, so..." I stood there waiting for her to budge, but she remained silent. "Umm, hello? Is anybody home?" I asked.

"Just close the fucking door, Rae!" She screamed the 'Rae', which signified she was pissed because she rarely called me Rae. It was always G, Genie, or Gene Rae Roman if she wanted me to know she was serious. But seldom ever Rae.

I stormed out of the bedroom and headed back upstairs. As I plated the food, I guess Boss could feel the tension in the air as I forcefully maneuvered the dishes and boxed food around.

"Yo, Boogie. What's the deal?" Boss stood there, unsure whether to sit down and eat or just leave. "Shorty living here now?" he asked hesitantly.

Then I exploded. "Tell me right now! Did you sleep with my best friend?"

"NO! Are you kidding me? Did she tell you that shit?"

"I'm just trying to figure out what all these years of tension have been about between you two," I said, leveling my tone.

"Look…I can leave now that I've caught up with you and see that you are okay. You know what, yeah, I'm just gonna dip. My bad for popping up on you unannounced, but now I know you're doing okay… I'm staying at the Biltmore and will be here until Sunday. I got your number back, and I promise to keep it near me. But the worst-case scenario, I do know where you live, and where your parents live too." He smiled, embracing me once more before he departed. "Before I leave, I have to ask…" he said, pausing.

"¿Qué pasa, Jefé?" I said sharply.

"Can I get a doggie bag?" he asked with uncertainty.

I shook my head at him and laughed. "Of course, you can!" I guess Jessie could feel Boss's departure because she stomped back upstairs immediately when he exited.

"Your lil' friend gone already?" she teased. I refuse to give her the silent treatment. "Jessie, let's talk," I said gingerly. She began plating her duck.

"Jessie, look at me," I said sternly.

She kept plating her duck when I snatched the takeout box from her hand, and she snapped. I knew that would stop the foolishness because she didn't mess around when it came to her food. "I want you to tell me what happened between you and Boss before this day is over." She sat at the end of the table, which now seemed unofficially labeled as Jessie's seat. I finished fixing her plate and placed it in front of her. I sat at the other end of the table and waited for her to start.

"Do you remember when I worked in that joint Boss had in Harlem for a brief spell?" I shook my head yes. "One day, when I got to work, Boss was there, which was rare. He pulled me aside and told me a client wanted to arrange a private dance for his friend's bachelor party in the Champagne Room. Look, I was old enough to know what was expected when someone was asked to go into the Champagne Room. I told him I would agree only if he promised to talk to him beforehand and let him know it would only be a dance, nothing else. He said the guy was a friend of one of his old college buddies who was getting married. He was a stand-up guy who wanted one last lap dance before his big day. He had come to the club once before and saw me, and I guess he liked what he saw. His fraternity brothers arranged with Boss to host his bachelor party at the club. Anyway, everything was going smoothly until more guys in his party found their way to the Champagne Room..." She went into the kitchen and grabbed the remaining Hennessy. She chugged it, paused long, and started eating again.

"Ah, hello, you got me on the edge of my seat." In response, she began sobbing hysterically. She couldn't even swallow the duck she was steadily shoving in her mouth. Jessie started to choke. I went over and rubbed and patted her back. She was still trying to eat.

"Jessie, stop eating, please, and release the trauma you've been holding onto all these years. I promise I'm here and will always have your back, no matter what. Just take some deep breaths. That's it…."

She slowly chewed and then swallowed the food. She began to breathe.

"Just release the memory. Let it go." I said, sounding like a shaman.

"Well, some of the men in the groom-to-be party entered the room and started asking me to give him sexual pleasure.

They were pressuring me to suck his cock. When I told them that I was only giving a private show to the groom and that they needed to leave, they became rude and touchy. Two of them ripped my G-string off and forcefully straddled me on the groom's lap. Then surrounded me in a tight circle so I couldn't move," she paused and took a deep breath.

"They were shouting, 'suck them big titties, Lee, suck them big titties, Lee.' He was so wasted he just went along with whatever they suggested," Jessie's voice quivered and creaked as she revealed her truth.

"I started to scream, and the bouncer came in and punched a guy with a condom halfway on. I didn't even notice him standing behind me with all the chaos. It was so dark and scary. I tried to muster all my strength inside and run away, but I couldn't move. I couldn't move at all." She stared quietly.

"Oh, my goodness, J," I said, tearing up. "What did management do about it?" I sat by her side.

"You know, G, it's all a part of that life. I'm not green. I know it's what I signed up for. Management gave me that half-assed reassurance, claiming those men would never be allowed entry into the club. About three weeks later, I saw Lee, who had just gotten married, taking off his wedding ring and going into the Champagne Room with another dancer."

"Did you inform security that the asshole was back?" I asked her.

"No. I knew then that no amount of money in the world was worth my peace of mind or dignity. I took it as a lesson learned and never went back."

"Does seeing Boss…I paused. "Triggered you?"

"Yeah, I guess it did."

"Oh, Jessie, I'm so sorry this happened to you, girl. Even after all these years, this wound still hasn't had a chance to heal. It has fragmented a piece of your mind. Too many women have these stories, and I hate that you're part of that painful statistic. You know what? You need to call your energy back! I understand—trauma and pain—things that hurt us can be hard to forget when scars are left behind. If you let trauma fester inside you for too long, it will drain your light completely. You're too incredible to let gross and disgraceful men like that damage your soul. You are stronger than this. Have you ever shared this story with anyone else? I can't believe Boss would have his name attached to such shitty work practices." I was getting heated.

"Genie, all management will have us do is fill out an incident report and ask if we want to report it to the police — yes or no. I didn't want to relive it. I just wanted to forget it ever happened, so I said no. Not even sure if Boss knows; he probably does, though. Other than that, no, not the girls who worked that night, not my parents, not even you — and you're my best friend. I genuinely know that Boss isn't the one to blame. And you're right. Seeing him reminds me of memories I wish I had never lived. He was never there, and management used to let all kinds of shit slide. But that's what you sign up for with that kind of life."

I interrupted her, "That gives them no fucking right to do what they did to you, J!"

"Yes, yes, it does…" she croaked, starting to whimper again. "Everyone knows what happens and what is expected when you go into that room."

"Maybe when you're grown and consenting, but that's different from some assholes forcing you to do unwanted things, trying to satisfy their perversions. And Boss was allowing this shit?"

"Nah, he was just the owner, the name. Boss's number one rule was, 'Don't get my shit shut down.' But you know how that business goes, everybody's hands in somebody's pocket. Plus, some dancers were accepting of those types of customers because they would make extra money under the table," she explained.

"Damn, why didn't you feel like you could tell me this before now?" I asked her.

"Because it was fucking embarrassing and traumatizing. It still is. Plus, Boss was your man at the time, so I decided not to ruffle those feathers." She sank into her seat, staring at her half-eaten duck.

"It's so terrible how many women become victims of sexual assault, but they don't tell anyone or report it to the police, just accept all the guilt and shame because of some incompetent bastard's mama or daddy issues. Entering that room did not give them the warrant to do whatever they pleased, and I hope you can find it in yourself to understand that. I see you are harboring some major trauma from this experience. Do you think you're ready to begin the healing process?"

She looked me in the eyes and nodded.

"I can book an appointment with my therapist. Would you like that?" I waited for her response. "You're right, G. I've been holding onto this for so long, and I thought I had let it go, but seeing Boss today just reignited the fact that it's still eating away at me. And no, Boss is not solely to blame, but when I saw that man back at the club weeks later, I felt as though they were conspiring. You know that old saying, *Bros before Hoes*, Boss…he was just the easiest target." She put her head on the table. "Do you want me to reheat your food?" I asked her.

"No, I'm not even hungry anymore." She picked up her head and plate and took them to the kitchen. I followed her and gave her an unannounced hug.

"Love you, girl. You're not alone, J. I'll do everything I can to help you through this."

"Can you promise me just one thing, Genie?"

"Anything."

"Other than the people who unfortunately know this information, promise you won't tell anyone else what happened to me. I want to bury this secret for good."

"Can you keep a secret?

"What's the secret?" she asked, leaning in.

"Sorry, I'm a Scorpio. I never share secrets," I whispered.

Our loud laugh broke through the silence of the dark conversation.

"I love you, girl."

"I love you too. I got your back forever."

   THE DREAM LIFE

CHAPTER 21

Soulmate of my dreams

Imet up with Boss at the Old Lady Gang Southern Cuisine restaurant for an early dinner before his flight. Of course, I had to defend my best friend's honor and reprimand him for neglecting his business practices, leaving out the sordid details. Although he usually becomes defensive when given constructive criticism, he immediately folded like a deck of cards and called her to apologize. He also booked Jessie a spa day at The Wellness Spot and ordered her an edible arrangement, all before we got our food. "Now that that's settled, I want to talk about you,

Ms. Roman. Boy, life-changing events can make you rethink your commitments," he shared.

"True. Just curious to know, how does my awful incident make you rethink your commitments?" I pondered aloud.

"Well, the fact of the matter is I knew from the moment I laid my eyes on you that you were my soulmate, Boogie-Down…" he paused, and I interjected.

"Pardon me? ¿Qué pasa con la Señorita Cubana?" Boss then came back at me with something I would rarely hear from his mouth, even when we were dating.

"I love ya, Boog. I know we would never work well in a man-woman, husband-wife capacity, you dig, but there's some reason why we've kept in contact all these years. You are my forever soulmate. You are the only person who knows how to put me in my place, and I respect you and what you have to say. I don't care who or what comes or goes. Whoa! Feels good to get that off my chest finally." I was so blown away by his confession that I couldn't even retort. We sat silently for a minute, then our food arrived.

"Oh, that looks good," I said, sticking my fork into his salmon without permission.

"You remember that I always hated it when you did that, right?" he said, giving me a look.

"Yep, but I'm your soulmate, remember, so deal with it." We laughed. Just as I was about to bite into my dessert, I felt a touch on my shoulder. I turned around, and there, standing, was Pablo.

"Pablo! Hi." I couldn't find any more words.

"Hey, Ms. Rae Roman. Good to see you. I've been calling you, but I see why you've been ducking me now." He looked

     THE DREAM LIFE

at Boss, who didn't even come up for air from the delicious, blackened salmon he was devouring. Then Boss's focus was broken by the words,

"Excuse me, Will, is it?" he blurted out. Boss gave him a confused look,

"Nah, not Will," he said rudely, continuing to eat.

"Boss, this is Pablo tha Picasso. The music artist I told you about." Boss gave a little nod. "Oh, my bad, I assumed you were the boyfriend. Can I speak with you alone for a quick sec?" Pablo said, making a head gesture toward the exit. We sat outside on the empty patio. "Look, Rae, I get it. You have a lot going on, and you're a busy businesswoman, but I can't help that I've fallen in love with you. I think, no, I know that you're my soulmate." I stood there stunned as the second man today, whom, I remind you, wasn't my man at all, was professing that he loved me, and I was his soulmate. How flipping ironic!

Pablo continued to assert his emotions. "And now I see you out with some other guy, and you can't even call me back. I know I wasn't the only one feeling a connection between us." I stayed silent. "Listen, Jessie said you wanted out of your contract, and I understand why. You're catching feelings for me, too, aren't you?" He paused for a reply. *Damn, now I have to answer,* I thought. My head, heart, or stomach was nowhere near ready for this unsolicited interruption from my meal, and now my food was getting cold.

"Pablo, I'm sorry, but things between us… You and I…Fuck it. Yes! Yes, okay! I was feeling you, too. However, my life is too much of a jigsaw puzzle to try to add another piece right now." I began to cradle myself and shiver. He took off his jacket and wrapped it around me. I gave him an uncomfortable look. I thought I would rather go back inside the warm restaurant than sit out here beating a dead horse. Yeah, so what? I found him attractive in more ways than one, but it wasn't a good time and probably never would be. "Listen, Pablo," I said, beginning to unwrap his jacket from around me. "Who knows what time will reveal. Maybe next lifetime. Okay?" He then leaned over and planted a kiss on my cheek. I moved my face away to dodge it. "Rae, did the assault not prove to you that life is too short to be straddling the fence when it comes to matters of the heart?" And with that, Pablo finished what he had to say and walked away. He went back inside to rejoin his crew sitting at a large table, and I went back to discover that Boss had eaten a portion of my shrimp po'boy. I gave him the squinty eyes and a furrowed brow.

He defended his actions with, "Doesn't feel so good when someone picks off your plate, does it?" I smiled it off and sat to finish the half-eaten, now cold meal. "Yo Ma, that's the kid you told me about?" Trying to chew down the large bite I took, I nodded yes.

"Everything's good with you two?" I'm not sure if he was trying to make small talk or pry, but I didn't want to engage or think about it.

"We're good," I said, managing the hard bread with my choppers.

"This kid got some balls to come over here and try and check you. Talkin' 'bout this must be Will. Nah, B. He must be feeling you, huh?" he said, continuing to pursue the topic. I

THE DREAM LIFE

remained quiet as I looked for the waiter to order the blackened salmon to go, but Boss just wouldn't let up. "If Will were still your man, I wondered how he would have handled that situation. Gotta another brother trying to check yo girl while we're eating. Men today don't have no code." His obsessive nature would stew in this situation all night if you let him. I finally couldn't take it anymore.

"Just drop it, Boss," I said firmly, "and what do you mean if Will was still my man?" I asked authoritatively. Between the unwanted interruption from Pablo, my cold meal, and Boss trying to instigate, I was getting aggravated.

"Oh, you still fucking with money? For real? Y'all must have an open…" he paused, then said, "You know what, that ain't my business."

"Nah, speak up. What is it?" He held his hand in the air for the non-existent waiter and said, "Check, please."

"Boss, it's against the rules to hide something from your soulmate," I warned him.

"My name is Bennett and ain' in it." He smiled. I frowned.

"Come on, Boss. What were you leading up to say?" He teased,

"Nah, it's bro code, Boog. Sorry." That infuriated me immediately. "Fuck that Bros before Hoes shit, which still got my best friend traumatized 'til this day! Tell me what you know, NOW!" All the sound in the entire restaurant came to a standstill for a brief moment as everyone turned and looked at us.

"OKAY, OKAY, calm down, sweetheart," he said, waving at me as if I were too hot.

"Don't patronize me, Boss. I'm not your sweetheart. Get to the point, already."

"Okay, Boogie-Down, damn." He took a long sip of his beverage and said, "Psych. I'm not telling you shit. That's y'all's drama to deal with." The waitress was back.

"How's everything? Would you all like to order dessert?"

"No, thank you," I said bluntly.

"Nah, Ma, it's time for me to jet out soon, so no dessert for me. Can I have a sweet tea to go, though?"

"Sure." She placed the bill on the table and scurried away. I stared at Boss with a scornful look. He began to laugh. "You mad tight, huh?" I was so annoyed with him that I decided to dismiss myself and head for the door. When I reached the curb to order an Uber, Pablo reappeared. "Rae, what's wrong? Is that guy bothering you?" I ignored his presence and continued trying to locate a car.

"Damn, twenty minutes!" I said to myself, wishing my exit could be swifter.

"Rae, talk to me, please. I can have my driver take you home if you want. It's no problem. He can swing back to scoop us later. We haven't even ordered yet," Pablo kindly offered. My head was starting to feel light and dizzy. As I swayed, Pablo caught me and led me to a bench. I suddenly felt nauseated.

"Yo, Boogie…Boog." I could hear Boss calling for me, but I was too disoriented to respond. Then I heard Pablo attempting to come to my defense.

"What the hell happened? What did you do to her?"

Boss's response was ever so uptown. "Yo, son. You bugged out! Dead all dat! Yo, Boog, you aight?"

            THE DREAM LIFE

"Nah, cuz, you got me fucked up if you think you're gonna do my girl like…." Pablo stated. Boss interrupted with a sarcastic laugh, "Yo girl? Me and shorty go way back, chump, so you need to step before I have to get gully with you." At that point, I felt myself falling to the ground, and everything was turning dark.

In an instant, Boss scooped me up like a knight in shining armor. As he speedily drove his rental back to my place, I felt like we were moving in slow motion. Words weren't clear. My head was pounding. His voice echoed in my head, but everything was choppy. "Boogie, hospital, breathe, love, get up." Suddenly, everything faded to black.

GENE ROMAN

CHAPTER 22

The Dream Team

When I came around, I could hear voices whispering loudly. I was feeling dazed and had a pounding headache and stiff neck. I had made it back home and was lying in my bed. How did I get here? I slowly started to blink. The light in the room felt like burning coals in my eyes, so I closed them and tried to recognize the voices. The first voice was, without a doubt, Jessie's. She seemed to be upset.

"If you don't tell her, I will."

"Tell me what?" I asked.

"Rae! Oh, thank God!" I heard her say.

"J. Please turn the lights off," I pleaded.

"How do you feel, Boogie?" *Boss?* I thought. *What was he doing here?*

"What are you doing here, Boss?" I said, finally opening my eyes completely to gather what exactly was transpiring.

"What you mean, Ma? I've been with you most of the day." My words seemed to frighten them both. Jessie looked at him. He looked at her.

"Can someone please tell me what the hell is going on? Why are you all in my bedroom? What are you guys whispering about? And now giving me nutty looks...." I asked straight out.

"Honey, it's okay. Calm down. Now, what's the last thing you remember?" Her mothering tone frustrated me even more.

"Please don't talk to me like I'm a child. What is going on? Tell me now!" When I said, 'tell me now,' the memory of everything came rushing back. I looked at Boss.

"You!" I screamed at him.

"Hol' up, Ma, you need to chill before you black out again." He walked over to Jessie and turned his back to me, "Shorty, we need to call the doctor or take her to the hospital," he whispered to her.

"Boss, you know your big mouth can't whisper. I remember exactly what happened. I'm feeling a bit confused and fuzzy from this migraine. Now, what is this bit of information my best friend and wannabe soulmate is keeping at bay?" I said, staying on the topic.

"Genie, what's important is that you're awake and remembering things now. I think you should go to the hospital to get yourself checked out," Jessie said in the most caring voice she could muster.

"Save the pity, okay J… You're hiding something from me, and that's not cool. Boss, what is the problem? You started all this drama at the restaurant, now spill the gatdamn beans," I demanded.

"Rae, you okay?" I heard a voice from outside.

"Who the hell is that?" I asked, sitting up and holding my head, which felt double in size.

"Pablo. He had his driver follow you all back here after all the commotion at the restaurant," Jessie responded.

"All what commotion?" I asked her. She looked at Boss again. "You know what. Y'all can stop it with all the eye messages and talk directly to me. I promise I can handle it."

"Well, clearly you can't, Genie. Something is going on with your head right now, and that's more critical than some bullshit," Jessie said, placing an ice pack on my head. I slapped it out of her hand. She then gave me; the *I know this bitch didn't* look.

"I'll tell you what. I'm going to the bathroom. When I come out, have the explanation ready or get to stepping and take Pablo with you." I stayed in the bathroom a little longer and tried to gather my memories. What was happening to me and why? The doctor told me that my memory could be affected for life because of the trauma caused during my attack. I was always someone who was in control of my life and its direction. Now it felt weird having people shelter my feelings and pity me because I couldn't remember anything. I remember getting angry with Boss, and Pablo was there. They got into it,

          THE DREAM LIFE

and then what? As I exited the bathroom, the two of them were still standing in the same spot as if glued to the floor.

"Okay. I'm assuming this indicates that you all are ready to apprise me as to whatever this dramatic information is that you feel I can't handle for some reason." I stood quietly, waiting for the grand reveal.

"Sit down, Boogie," Boss said, walking over and sitting on my chaise. He began, "First of all, I apologize. I didn't mean for you to get so irate and lose consciousness and all that shit. You know I'm always here for you, shorty…."

"Get to the damn point, Boss!" I shouted at him.

"Boss saw Will at the hotel with…." Jessie started to reveal the secret, but she stopped and looked at him. He shook his head as he cradled his face in his palms. He started again, "Okay, yes, I saw your dude with some chick, but as I told your homie, that doesn't mean shit. I honestly didn't even know you still fucked with him. That's why I was clownin' around at the restaurant." I composed a stream of questions as if I already had them written on note cards.

"Where and when was this? Did you recognize her? How does she look? Did it look like business, friendly, or more than that was going on?" He executed his responses flawlessly.

"At this restaurant near the Hudson, about four months ago, when I flew back to the States on business. No, I didn't recognize her. She looked like a model type—tall as hell, tanned skin, long blonde hair—a real Giselle-type chick. Shorty was bad for real! To me, it seemed like someone he was holding rather than a business meeting. However, I could be wrong. You know… perception can be a muthafucka…."

Then Jessie chimed in. "G, you know precisely who he's talking about. That white bitch Cindy!" Yep, I sure did. But my head was in dire pain. They were right. I really couldn't handle anything else at the moment, especially some news that my lover could be creepin' around with a woman who despised me.

This explained the strange vibe I had picked up during our Thanksgiving trip to Charleston. He seemed distant, like something was bothering him. Come to think of it, he's been distant and hard to reach lately. Will and I had promised each other that our relationship would be different this time. We promised to cut the infidelity out of the scenario so we could rebuild our trust and hopefully become husband and wife one day. We're both living the dream life. We are now where we had aspired to be and are highly successful at what we do. Nothing was holding us back but fear of our previous capricious ways. Now, to be back at square one was an arrow through my heart. I sat on my bed, motionless and speechless.

"Now, Boogie, I don't want you to jump to conclusions until you talk to the brother," Boss suggested. In my heart of hearts, I didn't need any confirmation. My intuition told me it was true. It was like when a detective is trying to solve a case, and that one missing piece of the puzzle has finally been exposed. That was the feeling that had been churning in my belly for longer than I wanted to admit.

"You okay, girl?" my bestie asked delicately.

"I will be."

With those concluding words, I took some pills the doctor prescribed for pain and headaches and bid them goodnight. Following their departure from my bedroom, I grabbed my

     THE DREAM LIFE

phone and called Will on impulse. I wasn't ready to reckon with the truth, but the impulsiveness took the lead. The phone rang and rang. I guess doubling the recommended dosage that I hadn't taken the first time, since getting the prescription filled, caused me to instantly drift off to the ringing on Will's end, which never connected, and if it did, I was out like a light.

I woke up around 9 p.m., sweating and feeling clammy. I stepped into my shower and turned the nozzle to my favorite setting. The water felt like a real waterfall pouring down on my head, reminding me of the intense migraine. I wouldn't dare turn on a light with the pain that had numbed my frontal cortex earlier. Using only the dim glow from a salt rock lamp on the bathroom vanity, I felt my way around the shower, which seemed surprisingly larger at that moment, to find my shampoo and conditioner. Now feeling refreshed, I sat down, gathering my thoughts and feelings.

I wanted a more profound understanding of how I felt about this allegation. I wanted to feel all the feelings to have a clear head and not get immediately irrational when I addressed Will. I mean, this was from Boss's perspective, after all. Though in my heart, I felt it was true. If indeed Will did confess to creepin' with whoever, does this mean I'm done with him for good this time? If I decided to stay, would I have the strength to rebuild trust with him all over again? Then I contemplated, what if he admits to cheating and it's a loophole to not be with me anymore, and he's been hoping he would eventually get caught? Damn, what is the lesson from this shit show? First the attack, now Boss's revelations that Will is possibly, maybe, hopefully not doing me dirty. At that moment, I shifted my focus to a mountain. "I'm a strong mountain. A giant that can withstand much force...I cannot be moved. I will stand firm on my Earth. I'm a strong mountain. A giant that can withstand...."

Then the *knock, knock, knock interference* landed on my bathroom door.

"What's up?" I asked of the unexpected intruder.

"Yo ma, you good in there?" Boss's NYC accent had never been easier to decipher.

"I'm fine," I said, short on tolerance.

"Aight. Let me know if you need anything," he said confidently. Why was he still here? Hadn't he shaken things up enough since his arrival?

All I need for him to do is leave already, I thought. I brought myself back to my center and began meditating again. I tapped on my Tibetan singing bowl to dive into a deeper vibration. Breathing in and out with 10-second counts, I refocused on my third eye vision. I was on top of my mountain, finding my clarity in all this. I quickly dismissed the displaced anger I wanted to project onto Boss. He was merely the messy messenger.

A memory of my parents flashed through my mind. The endless love they appeared to share, even during times when they were separated by threats to their affection for each other. Over the years, they sometimes grew awkward around each other, as if they were strangers. Then, suddenly, they would remember their bond. They recalled that they had vowed to love each other for a thousand years. I thought this was the cycle of love that Will and I shared, too, but I began to doubt everything. Now, seeing my life playing out in routine, I yearn

   THE DREAM LIFE

for something more. Most times, our lives drift off course or get thrown around, guiding us back to our true destiny. I hate to admit that a blow to the head has forced me to reset and reevaluate my life, but it has, undeniably, done just that.

Yes, I have loved Will since junior high. Yes, I will always have a special love for him and pray that his life is well and fulfilled, but the emptiness of so much separation was starting to tear away at our chemistry. Work is work, and we decided to make our fortunes before making a family. That was our agreement from the beginning, but ultimately, the long distance and sacrifices set us up for traps on Temptation Island. I now realize this same notion was also informing the companionship between Pablo and me. However, there are always three sides to a story. One is the truth, and that's the only one that deserves my attention.

After my meditation, I prayed and got dressed. I stopped jumping to conclusions and called Will again. No response. I thought, no big deal but also wondered, hmm, why hasn't he made an effort to return my calls? I left my room for the terrace to get some fresh air. To my surprise, I found Boss and Jessie sitting around the fire pit. "Well, well..." I said, sliding the door open. "I assume this means the long-lasting feud is finally over? At last, some good news!" I looked at the two of them, and they looked at each other, then looked back at me. Laughter erupted.

"Oh! Y'all smoked a *J,* and that solved everything, huh?" They continued to rotate the mirth-inducing joint that had bonded them in their newly found friendship. I went back inside to order them some takeout since I knew they would try to come back in and raid a mostly empty fridge. *I desperately need to have some essentials and groceries delivered,* I thought, as I scrolled on Door Dash for tonight's vittles. Jessie had been doing the shopping, but work had been nonstop for her lately, so we've been heavily chowing down on Atlanta's takeout scene. Yep, it had been all work and no play for us. I couldn't remember the last time we had had a bar-hopping night of debauchery. That's it! I must stop living for the few seconds I shoot in photos, trying to capture lasting memories, but live wholly in every second, of every breath, enjoying every moment. Not just for the perfectly filtered shots, but for the moments that are out of focus and blurred, as they also vividly define my story.

CHAPTER 23

"*Dream until you're ready*

to wake up and face reality

of what the truth is."

-C.K.B.

I checked back into the physical realm and went to retrieve my phone to try and get Will on the line. I didn't know what I wanted to say to him, only that I needed to hear his voice. At first, he had been so adamant about finding the perpetrators who put me in a coma. Now he seemed to have fallen off the map. I knew the accusations could have engendered these newfound feelings, so I tried to dismiss them quickly. But hell, a girl's only human, right? As I entered my passcode, Boss yelled, "Yo, Boog! The food here!"

"Okay. I'm on the phone," I hollered back. I sat there listening to the ringtone. As it constantly rang, I began to feel angry. I clicked it off as his voicemail started to play. He has some nerve ignoring my calls and not taking the time to return my call. Right then, I wished I could see and talk to him. If only he were within driving distance. Then I thought… Boss was flying back into New York on a private jet. I could hitch a flight and confront Will face to face. I walked out of the bedroom to join them around the dinner table.

"How are you feeling, Genie?" Jessie asked immediately.

"A little numb, but what are you gonna do?" I said, hopelessly shrugging my shoulders.

"Hey, Boss." I paused and didn't say anything, trying to see how to ask for a free flight to NYC.

"Hey," he replied, giving me a go-on nod.

"Is there spare room on the jet for your old buddy, old pal?"

He started eating again and then replied, "That depends. Is this old buddy, old pal trying to start some shit?" His eyebrows shot up to show my uncertainty. "Aye, B, I'm truly sorry for all the drama I caused today. For real, ma, I really, really am, but there's no way in hell I'm going to condone you starting some shit with that man after how your head was trippin' today. Shorty, you buggin' B. Just go chill somewhere. Get ya head right, fuck ya heart right now. You and ya homegirl can go jump him later when you get ya mind right first, for real." After his little speech, I told him, "That's fine… you're entitled to your opinion. However, I was asking because it would have been less stressful to fly on a private flight, but Delta will do," I said nonchalantly and started to eat.

Boss caved. "Okay. Okay. Damn, B, I'll see to it that you get to ya man in one piece. But promise me you're not going up there to get arrested or some shit…."

"If she does, I'll be right there with the bail money," Jessie chimed in.

"Thanks, J! And Boss, you can go to hell, respectfully. But only after this flight to New York. How old do you think I am? I'm far from that little, teenybopper you thought you knew years ago, who would fight those lil' hoes that would come at me left and right about you. I'm too booked and busy to have time to go to jail over a disgruntled love affair. By the way, I have a meeting with L'Oréal this coming week in Manhattan, so this works out perfectly," I said confidently, burying potential pain in my subconscious and focusing on the parts of me that I could control.

"Are you going to call him before you come?" Jessie asked me.

"I've been calling him. He's not answering. I haven't talked with him in four days," I revealed. All you could hear for a moment was the sound of chewing, then Jessie added more script to keep the plot building. "So, how are you planning to approach him with this situation?"

I let out a long sigh and said, "I don't know."
Jessie left me a note on my luggage with a cute quote about girl power. She apologized again for not being able to accompany me to the confrontation. She made it sound like an episode of Cheaters when the host takes the poor victim to

pop up on the infidel for the big 'I caught you red-handed' moment. When we arrived in NYC, Boss had two cars waiting, one for him and one for me.

"Now, are you sure you don't want me to come with you for moral support?" he asked sarcastically.

"Thanks, Boss, but you'll be the last person I'll ever lean on for moral support."

"Yeah, that's probably best," he responded, laughing.

On the way to Will's new condo—or extended-stay placement, as his firm called it—I decided to phone him once more. And would you believe it, he answered!

"Hello, my love!" he answered, sounding way too chipper for me.

"Oh, don't hello my love me! Where have you been? Visiting Venus?" My dander was most definitely up.

"No, but we can put it on our list of places to visit soon. Why so testy, Rae?" I couldn't believe he had the nerve to question my attitude after almost a week of avoidance.

"Will, you buggin'! How do you have the gall to act like you haven't been ducking and dodging my calls left and right?" I was huffing mad. I could tell the driver was annoyed by the earful of someone else's dirty laundry from the faces he was making in the rearview mirror.

"Rae, calm down. You don't want to add extra stress to those healing wounds." By offering this advice, Will made it clear how out of touch we were. My head and heart had been in panic mode for a while since returning home from rehab. I held back from cursing at him over the phone. I wanted to save it all for an all-out confrontation—face-to-face, with the chance to roll my neck and wave my hands. We hadn't argued

THE DREAM LIFE

much over the years. However, my tongue-lashing game was unbeatable when it was in effect. I often teased him about this because, even though I switched my major from law to business, and Will continued, he would say no judge or jury would grant him a win against my argumentative ability. He was a Cancer and I was a Scorpio, so our personal beliefs ran ocean deep. However, I would warn him, even though we both had claws, only I had venom. He'd usually concede and say, 'I rest your case, your honor,' during heated moments.

"Where…are…you?" I asked very sharply.

"I'm coming out of the gym at the condo. About to go shower, then grab some dinner," he replied, relaying his plans to me.

"Oh, dinner, huh? Okay, great, maybe we can eat together for a change. Since I'm in…." Just as I started to let him know I was nearby, there was a burst of static, and the call dropped. I saw that the phone went back to the home screen. I then tried FaceTiming him, but it didn't connect. I figured I was in a drop zone.

"Damn technology," I said aloud. The driver sighed with relief after the phone call ended.

We pulled up in front of the high-rise moments later. The driver swiftly came around to open my door. He quietly assisted me by carrying my Louie to the entrance. I pulled a Benjamin out and handed it to him.

"Thank you," I said, expressionless.

His face brightened. "Oh, thank you, Miss! You have a blessed day!" he said, tipping his hat to me. I walked over to the concierge to summon Will.

"Hello. Can you tell me where I can find William Jones?" The person behind the desk didn't look up; she seemed to be taking lunch or having a snack.

"Is he expecting you?" she asked, without taking her eyes off the small TV she was watching.

"Yes," I lied. She then rolled her chair over to the computer.

After a few clicks, she said, "He's on the 12th floor. Unit 1206. Press the green button for the elevator foyer door to unlock." She rolled back to the TV.

I did as I was directed, and in the blink of an eye, I was at his door. Truth be told, I felt the stress weighing me down. I wanted Will to reassure me that Boss had it all wrong. Followed by intense makeup sex to put the drama all behind us. However, once the door opened and I saw his face, I wanted to scream "traitor" at him.

"Oh, my goodness! What a surprise! Why didn't you tell me that you were in town on the phone?" After giving him a cold hug, I walked around the condo, surveying things he couldn't have cleaned up due to my unannounced visit. The bedroom was the first stop. He came in and asked, "Are you looking for something?"

"More like someone!" I came right out with it. I refuse to let an elephant occupy the space. Will was one guy I could easily catch in a lie because he would give himself away with his shifty gestures and stuttering.

"When is the last time you saw Cindy?" I asked. He looked at me sideways.

"Huh?" he responded. I didn't even repeat the question; I just paused for his brain to catch up to what I had asked.

"If you can 'huh', you can hear," I said, continuing to scavenge the place.

"What in the hell? What's up with you, Rae?" he asked, playing the dumbfounded role.

"Look, just answer the damn question!" I stated firmly.

"Did she bring some drama and lies to one of your photoshoots again?" he replied, continuing to deflect. I plopped down on the gray leather couch, folding my arms and crossing my legs.

"When was the last time you saw her?"

"Well, funny, you should ask. I bumped into her at this restaurant by the bay. She was solo. I was solo…."

"And your dick was solo, so she just decided to call shotgun!"

"What? No! We had a meal together, that's it. It was just a coincidence."

"After all the drama she's caused in the past. After I told you about the drama at my shoot? I can't believe you right now!" I would typically walk away when I felt my emotions were riding too high, but this time I faced them and him head-on.

"I'm sorry if you feel slighted by us coincidentally being at the same place at the same time, and we both happened to be eating at the bar. I mean, she sat there and ordered her meal. I ordered mine. We chatted a bit and walked out together. It wasn't like I called her up and said let's grab dinner. I'm sorry that this upsets you, but trust me, there was nothing to it…." he added, continuing to soothe his conscience by pleading. I eventually tuned into my own thoughts to decide if I believed any of his testimony. I also realized it stemmed from ideas Boss had put in my head, not knowing or recognizing his lousy history with that woman. Then I remembered that Boss himself had possessive traits toward me. It could have all been coming from jealousy. But yet and still, why had Will become so distant as of late? Not answering any calls or returning them. He most definitely is well-informed on the damage Cindy has caused in the past. I decided to let it go and believe Will's claims.

"Okay. Okay, if you said there's nothing to it. Fine," I said, throwing my hands up in defeat. "But I don't care if that wench just happens to stroll into McDonald's while you're in the middle of purchasing a Big Mac. Walk the other way. OKAY?" I stated definitively, warning him that there was a line he mustn't cross.

"Rae, don't be so insecure. She's not and will never be on your level," he said, as if I didn't know this.

"I know," I replied, short and sweet.

"How did you even know I saw her, though?" he questioned.

"Wouldn't you like to know?" I responded slyly.

As the darkness outside grew, New York City began to glow. My unexpected arrival was just in time because Will had finished closing a deal with a grueling client. He seemed happy about my visit, aside from the fact that I had initially come to wreck shit. He said he wanted to grab a shower and take me out on the town. While he was in the shower, my gut shouted loud and proud, "Go through his phone!" It was sitting right on the table. I reached to grab it, then I paused. I told myself, *you said you would let it go, Rae. You all talked. He's not ignoring*

     THE DREAM LIFE

you intentionally. He's a businessman. He has loads of responsibilities at work that demand attention. Just let it go. After talking myself off the edge of mistrust, I took off my clothes and headed to the shower to join Will for some passionate and steamy make-up sex. It began slowly with us bathing each other. But when he flipped me upside down, landing my mouth on his erect shaft and my cakes in his face, I knew he had been missing me for sure. After we had our way with one another, we exited the foggy bathroom to get ready for dinner.

We kept the bartender busy making us Old Fashioned cocktails as we waited patiently for our tables. A seemingly drunken older couple was at the bar celebrating their retirement by buying several shots for everyone around them, toasting to their escape from the rat race.

By the time we were seated, I felt quite nice and toasty. While reading the menu, trying to conjure up an appetite subdued by too many drinks, the room began to spin.

"Hey, Will," I said, planting my forehead on the white-cloth table.

"Yes, my love?" he asked, not taking his eyes away from the menu.

"Can we leave? I'm sorry, but I don't feel so hot all of a sudden." He looked at me and stood up, coming to pull my chair out so we could leave. The last thing I remember is him unzipping my black cocktail dress, easing off my Red Bottoms, and covering me with the comforter. He kissed me on my forehead and whispered, "I'm going to prepare my briefs for Monday. Get some rest."

CHAPTER 24

Dream life comes crashing down

I woke up around 5 a.m. feeling like I had been hit by a freight train. "Oh no!" I yelled and ran into the bathroom to release the poison juices consumed hours ago.

"Oh, Gawd! Why did I drink so much?" I asked myself, feeling just terrible. Since the attack, I hadn't been partaking in libations as much as in the past, and it showed. My body rejected every bit of alcohol I swallowed at that swanky bar. Finally, I felt depleted from the regurgitation, so I trekked across the cold stone floor in the living room to lie on the gray leather couch. At least if more came, it would be easier to clean here than in the carpeted bedroom. I also grabbed the lined trash can from the bathroom, just in case.

I jumped up, dazed and confused, when I awoke for the second time. I had forgotten where I was. I looked around the desolate gray condo. There was no sign of Will. As I was about to get my phone from the nightstand, I noticed it was already beside me on the couch, smushed into the cushion. When I attempted to pull it out, it fell farther back behind the couch cushions, which I noticed was also a pullout bed. "Oh, come on!" I said, already feeling defeated by my hangover. My head felt like someone was inside of it, beating my brain like a drum. I tossed the couch pillows off ferociously, trying to retrieve my phone. My eyes saw something that looked like a piece of ripped fabric nudged between the folds of the couch. It was too dark and gloomy to see, so I grabbed it and walked to the glass-paned wall. Were my eyes deceiving me? Had my drunkenness caused me to become delusional? I walked to the kitchen and turned on the light, revealing what I had assumed I was seeing. It appeared to be a bright red laced G-string. My head began to spin, and I ran into the bathroom to hurl again. After composing myself, I walked back to the torn-apart couch and got my phone to call Will. As the phone rang, I quickly hung up. In the heat of the moment, I was feeling too weak for that conversation, so I decided to get myself together and confront him in person. I wanted to see how quickly he could come up with a lie this time. I sat there fuming until I decided to let go of the negativity and work on my layout for my meeting with L'Oréal the next day.

The hours began to pass quickly. Then I started thinking. This is a rented condo; maybe the G-string was left here. There's no way he'd ruin what we had built all these years later.

I began to make excuses for Will in my mind, even though I hadn't yet discussed the issue with him. Then again, he's a man. I had to get out of my head and stop assuming. The sun's rays began to pierce the wall's window brightly, illuminating the once-dull, grayish apartment. I put on my workout gear and sneakers and decided to go for a run. Many people were outside enjoying the unusually warm weather for this time of year. Families were having picnics, kids were playing stickball, and older folks were arguing over a chess game. The aroma of street food filled the air. The Halal Guys had a line around the block. My stomach began to grumble. A knish would undo all the cardio I just did, but I didn't care. I stood in line for eleven minutes, and it was worth it. The knish was warm, flaky, and delicious. The filling was oozing out, just like I liked mine. On my walk back to the condo, I saw two police officers giving a man, who looked homeless, a hard time. One of the cops wheeled the homeless man's belongings to the trash can and started tossing them in.

"Hey, man! Would you like it if I came to your house and threw your shit in the damn trash?" the vagrant man yelled, questioning the out-of-line cop.

The cop just rudely responded, "It's just a bunch of trash, so that's where it belongs." My blood started to boil.

The other cop said, "How many times will we have to come down here and evict you? What, yo baby mama don't put up with your B.S. anymore? Taxpayers pay for the sidewalks to stay clean, not to be lined with bums." I wanted to stay out of it, but my conscience would not allow it.

"Excuse me, officers. What's the issue here?" I asked, interrupting their bully parade.

   THE DREAM LIFE

"Lady, mind ya business. This doesn't concern you," the jackass with the stereotypical cop mustache replied.

"Oh, but I believe it does. For one, I am a taxpaying citizen, and these are the sidewalks I pay taxes on as you mentioned…and I don't contribute to seeing innocent people ridiculed on these said sidewalks…."

"Are you done, lady?" the second cop interjected.

"Nope! So, as I was saying, I am a close friend of a closer friend to the senator of this great state, and I'm sure he would agree that taxpayers also pay for police to protect and serve, not bully and badger." They grew silent. I took out my phone and jotted down their names in my notes. I then turned on the camera because recording nonsense like this can sometimes be beneficial.

"Now, Officer Bryant, please retrieve this man's… I'm sorry, sir, what is your name?"

"My name is Thomas, but everyone calls me Tommy."

"Please retrieve Mr. Tommy's belongings from the trash and let me remind you that you are on camera if you would like to continue in the dishonorable manner in which you all started." You could tell he did not want to honor my request, but he looked at the phone, then reached over and pulled Tommy's collectibles out of the trash and placed them back in the shopping cart.

"Thank you. Officer Bryant. Officer Young. Do better. You never know who may be watching," I said, somewhat snarkily. Tommy and I stood our ground and watched as the unprofessional cops got into their squad car and drove off.

"Thank you, Miss…." he offered, waiting for a name.

"Rae," I responded.

"Those two jacks always seem to have a stick up their asses with me. They always throw my things in the trash…I can tell they would throw me in the trash if they could." Tommy's eyes welled up with tears. My heart broke for him.

"Would you like me to help you find a shelter?" I asked, my compassion rising to the surface. He turned away and began repacking his belongings. "Can I get you some items? Some food?" I asked.

He continued to rearrange his things. "Young folks like you give me hope that a better day will come. I respect you. Thank you for respecting me! Respect!" he said with a Jamaican accent, flashing me a peace sign. Tommy then strolled on down the avenue, humming Bob Marley's One Love song. And just like that…he kept on pushing. It was inspiring, to say the least. He didn't want pity or sorrowful tears; he wanted respect.

On my walk back to Will's condo, I reflected on what had just happened. I had long ago decided that respect was more than love. Thomas's outlook reminded me of that. I cared more for Will than I had for any past lovers. Sure, a few encounters with others had happened between us, but respect was always there. Will and I shared a unique understanding in this lifetime. We never believed that monogamy could be a real thing. Hence, how many people have multiple partners, multiple relationship statuses, and the undeniable stats of marriages ending in divorce. It's disheartening to consider how it all works. People spend years on dead-end relationships instead of admitting it's over. But I guess that's the price of betting on love. In the words of Jon Witherspoon, *"you win some, you lose some."*

Then there are those who find their true love, their soulmate—whether they act on it right away or not—the universe always seems to bring souls back together, and it's real. Those are the lucky ones.

It's all about discipline when it comes to this whole monogamy thing. Just the same as being disciplined with many things, such as finances, exercise, eating habits, etc. Being in a committed relationship seems to breed temptations from all four corners of the world. Hell, just thinking of some of the enticing moments Pablo and I shared would make me wet. I wasn't trying to make excuses for Will's fuck up if the allegations were factual; rather, I was attempting to reason with my own beliefs and not be so quick to judge him.

Why do we all strive for perfect monogamy or fairytale romance? I wanted to blame Western propaganda embedded in TV programming, although it could be due to our conformity to societal norms. It was more than likely just our innate desire to be nurtured after we exit our mother's comforting womb. Do I respect a man who pretends to be all mine and quietly cheats, or do I respect him more if he blatantly admits that he likes to roam the streets like an alley cat? The dangers of playing a love game of the multiples can get tricky, but I prefer the upfront version.

CHAPTER 25

"Hope is the dream of a waking man." –Aristotle

When I got back to the condo, I noticed the light was on in the bathroom.

"Will..." I called out, awaiting a response.

"Hey, Queen." It was the first time hearing him call me Queen that made my skin crawl. The uncertainty and the jealousy had taken hold. *Who else had he been calling Queen?* I pondered.

"How long are you going to be? We need to talk." I retorted.

"Oh shit...What did I do now, Rae?" he asked, replying with his typical response to we need to talk. I went into the guest bathroom to shower. When I returned to the living room, he was waiting with a beautifully wrapped box. Damn, I haven't even busted his chops, and he's already pulling out the makeup gifts. This gesture had the stench of guilt and deceit all over it.

I sat down beside him, unenthused. "What's this?" I asked dryly. He passed me the box. "Just a little sumtin' sumtin' for you, you sexy thing. I thought we could do a little role-playing tonight. You game, Cinnamon?" He had a dumb smirk on his face as if he thought this gift would override my 'we need to talk.' I slowly untied the neatly knotted pink velvet ribbon, then peeled off the velvety black damask wrapping paper. When I opened the box, I could not believe my eyes. Without thinking, I slapped Will with the box and red-laced G-string inside it.

"What the hell is wrong with you, Rae? Damn, the word is thank you, dammit!" I sat there, face to face, ready to go off on him something nasty. I now had the cold, hard evidence that he was the purchaser of the lacey red G-string I had stumbled upon earlier that day. But I was frozen. It was all too much at that moment.

"What did you slap me for? Why are you looking like that?" he asked, continuing to confront me with what was now feeling like an absurd line of questioning. I jumped up and went to the bedroom to get the other pair I had found tucked away inside the pullout couch. I charged back into the living room and threw the underwear on the table as if I was playing a guaranteed card in a game of Spades. At that moment, Will's face turned white like he had seen a ghost.

"So, I'm guessing I'm not the only Cinnamon you like to role-play with?" Silence blanketed the room for a whole minute before he responded with,

"Where did those come from?" I was expecting him to take the less hostile road of denial.

"Are you sure that's what you want to lead with? Shouldn't I be asking that question?" I asked loudly, angry bile now rising in my throat.

"Listen, Rae. I promise, baby. It was a stupid mistake…." he responded weakly, confessing to his scheming ways.

"You can't be serious! So, let me get this straight. You accidentally walked into Victoria's Secret and bought underwear for some woman to wear for you, then cheated on me while I've been dealing with all this trauma from the assault. Okay, then you were even more drunk or delusional when you thought it was okay to repurchase the same pair for me. What was that for? To mask your guilt and shame? Do you think I'm a fucking idiot? Put some respect on my name!" By then, I was pacing the floor, heated, ready to call the brothers I never had to kick his ass.

"Rae, please forgive me. It meant absolutely nothing to me. We have been doing so great, but I fucked up and let temptation get the best of me," he said, whining and pleading.

"Will, actively purchasing underwear for another woman is intentional, not a mistake!" I screamed.

"They were for you, Rae! I planned to surprise you in Atlanta one weekend, but my plans fell through…."

"Fell through or changed to fucking someone else?" I interjected.

"Please, just try to understand. I never meant to hurt you. One thing just led to another," he continued.

"Of course, you never meant to hurt me because you never meant for me to find out. I'll tell you. Everything happens for

     THE DREAM LIFE

a reason, and if Boss hadn't ever assumed he saw you with that skank, I wouldn't even be here to bring this revelation to light."

"Hold up. Boss! You mean to tell me that fat ass hating bully is the motive for why you're coming at me, all Billy Badass? Good to see he's still a hater. Were you with him?" He thought he was going to redirect the flame —oh no, buddy, not today.

"Aht-Aht! Don't even try to throw me in the heat with your ass! You've known for years that Boss and I still do business and are friends only—nothing romantic, all platonic. And don't pretend like it's something different now that your ass is sitting in the fire. Now the main question: who did you fuck? And do I know her?" The look on his face said it all. It was apparent, but I wanted him to confess. I needed to hear Will say her name.

"Can't we settle this between us? No one else has the right to correct this wrong for the dishonest, disrespectful, dirty shit I've done but me!" he cried, really thinking that putting it this way would convince me.

"Will, when a dog lies with other dogs sometimes, they contract fleas. So, yes, it matters who you lie with. Now tell me who she is before this gets bad for your temporary housing situation!"

"Okay. Damn, just chill! You calm?"

"Will, you deadass think I'm playing? You had enough balls to cheat on me after vowing to never again, now be man enough to admit with who!"

He started, "Well, I wasn't all the way frank about the night I ran into Cindy at the bar...."

Before he could finish, I charged at him with all my strength.

"You are a fucking two-timing bastard!" I screamed as I threw blows.

"First, you lie to my face after I blatantly ask you about her. Then, you have the nerve to buy the same cheap lingerie for me that you had that slut bouncing on your dick with?"

"I told you, I bought them for you. I felt so terrible about the whole thing. That's why I bought another pair. I thought it would ease my conscience and undo my wrong. You must believe me, Rae. I wanted to come clean, but didn't want to cause any more trauma to your healing. That shit meant nothing to me. I promise." He was crying at this point.

"Let me ask you a question. When I confronted you about her, why didn't you respect me enough to tell me the truth? You know secrets never sleep, forever…" I would have given him all the money in my bank accounts if he had answered this question truthfully, but instead, he gave me the sugar-coated lie.

"I didn't want to hurt you, Rae."

Men kill me. They keep the truth away because they don't want to hurt you, all while doing the same. Why say you don't want to hurt me? Just say, 'I hoped you would never find out about it.' *I didn't mean it, I promise, I'm sorry…* means absolutely nothing after the fact. Like Jessie says, "You can't do nothing once the snow has fallen. So why pretend to care now when you could have prevented the whole act?

I sat there quietly, listening to this grown-ass man cry and beg for forgiveness. Was he sorry about his actions when he brought her back to his place? No! Was he in this much agony and pain when he suggested she put on lingerie, allegedly purchased for me? No! Was he truthful when I asked him if he was seeing her again? I think not! My head started to throb as I thought of all the drama. I needed a makeover. I could not remember the last day I spent without a looming migraine, a pattern that was beginning to worry me. I knew they were a side effect of my injury, but this unnecessary drama wasn't exactly a blue pill. I needed a break from all this.

"Will, I know in the past we've done whatever we wanted to, but this time around, we agreed to be committed to each other. If I had known we were still on this path, I would have been…." I paused for a second as I was about to say, 'I would have screwed Pablo's sexy ass,' but I paused and processed what good that would do. I'm sure that, regardless of his infidelity, the double standards table would have been turned over if I had confessed to how many opportunities I dodged to stay committed to him. It's funny how a man never wants to hear or admit to himself that their woman also has dick options raining from the sky. The issue of cheating would go from being Will's drama to my drama if I even mentioned that I had prospects. Men have to be left in denial so their egos stay intact.

He interrupted the brief moment of silence. "If you had known, what would you have done? You've been seeing someone else, Rae?" he asked firmly. See how quickly he turned on the deflection?

"No," I responded. I was going to say I would have ended this, so you can still run the streets like the dirty dog you are." Then we sat there in what seemed like endless purgatory, not making any eye contact or gestures, just waiting to see who would break the silence.

Then he asked, "What are you thinking about?"

I wondered how many other women he had been involved with, but instead, I looked into his dishonest eyes and confessed, "I won't lie, Will, this really hurts, especially after we reestablished our commitment. And to think it was her, of all people—remember when she tried to undermine me at the photoshoot? You sleep with her months later, then gaslight me by saying I was insecure, knowing full well you were with her?" I muttered in frustration, a low groan escaping me.

"I'm going to leave now. I'll get a room somewhere else…."

He interrupted, saying, "No, Rae, you stay here. I will find somewhere else. It's my fault. I should have recognized the trap."

"The trap?" I responded, laughing hysterically, "Just stop. No one trapped you but you! And you think I want to stay here of all places? Imagining you banging that slut in the red laced thong meant for me! Well, allegedly meant for me." I stood up and began to pace the floor.

"Is this why you haven't been answering my phone calls or giving me any updates on what you found out about my attackers from your detective friend? Is there even a detective friend, Will, or is that just something that sounds good to help ease your guilt and cover up your no-good deeds?"

"Come on now, Rae, you know I know plenty of people in law enforcement. I've just been too busy with work lately."

"Yeah. Too busy working your way back between that no-talent having snow bunny's legs! You seriously allowed your

    THE DREAM LIFE

willpower to be compromised for a nut? I can't believe you jeopardized everything we've been working for." My blood was beginning to reheat. I wanted to pounce on him again, but instead, I composed myself, walked into the bedroom, and began packing up my things. He followed me into the room. "Listen, Rae, I know this is a fresh wound, but we will overcome this and be together. We cannot let this one fuck up damage what we've built. I understand you are angry, and I don't blame you. I will do whatever it takes to show you that you are the only girl who feeds my soul. You are my soulmate for life," Will took a breath, then paused. I suppose he was waiting for me to respond, but I refused, remaining silent instead.

"And yes, I'm still in contact with Detective Daniels about your case. If there was anything to report, trust me, you would know. My shortcomings have nothing to do with me finding out who hurt you. I promise you that! We are still going to find whoever did this to you, Rae." I was steadily and angrily tossing my things into my luggage.

"Rae, are you listening? Rae! Answer me, dammit!" I just ignored him, letting him say whatever he thought would soothe this low blow. Will despised the silent treatment. Although I felt betrayed, I could sympathize with his plight in this long-distance love affair, even though I would never admit it verbally. The miles apart and the countless lonely hours I spent wanting him to be in my bed at night, but he wasn't, I could sure understand how he took the fall. But with her?! How could he?!? He should have known better.

I lugged my Louie, now feeling twice as heavy, out of the bedroom. I felt so weak and faint that I could barely carry it. Somehow, I realized that this now seemingly overbearing luggage was the perfect allegory for the situation at hand. The weight of the fears and truths I had ignored or denied in my real life was manifesting in my ability to cross the threshold with baggage. My anxiety and fear held my mind hostage, as if the luggage was the problem because it was a burden to carry. However, it was my choice to carry the burden rather than let it go that kept me bound. All at once, I dropped my longtime vintage travel companion, Mr. Louie, to the ground, just as I had made the decision right then and there to drop the drama caused by my longtime sweetheart.

Maya Angelou once said, 'If you don't like something, change it. If you can't change it, change your attitude about it.' Will, here and now, I choose to drop the burdens and fears I can no longer tolerate or carry. I must change my attitude about our relationship. I can no longer be with you. It's over between us." After expressing these words, I crossed the door's threshold feeling light as a feather.

CHAPTER 26

Please be dreaming

"Hey, Ms. Rae Roman, with your fine self. You had me worried."

"And why is that, Raymond?" I asked dryly as I signed for the handful of packages the concierge desk had been collecting for me.

"You know, a brother needs his fix of your beautiful sight. You've been MIA lately. I thought you might have moved."

I continued to sign without giving him my full attention.

"Rae, are you okay?"

"Just dandy, Raymond. Have a nice day," I said, walking to the elevator with my arms full of packages.

"Oh, let me carry those to your condo for you."

"Thanks, but I think I can manage." In my mind, I was thinking he couldn't be serious. I'll never forget when he used the key I left at the desk for my parents, who were coming into town while I was flying out. He said it was because my neighbor smelled smoke coming from my condo. When I asked my neighbor about it, she claimed she only reported smelling smoke in the elevator foyer, not that it was coming from my place. He had given me the creeps ever since. That was the perfect opportunity to have him tossed. But management claimed they didn't have camera footage of him entering my condo. So, I added my own security cameras to my doors and inside my home, changed my locks, and never left a key at the desk again. I felt it'd be safer under a brick in Times Square than at the desk with Raymond. He was the kind of weirdo who would probably steal your unmentionables and wear them just to get off. I didn't care if I had to make several trips to bring my packages up. I didn't want his strange ass coming anywhere near my residence.

"Oh yeah, I forgot to give you this message. It's been here for about the last three days," he said, running over with an envelope in his hand.

I placed the packages on my foyer table and opened the note.

I came by your place today.
Come by the house as soon as you can.
-Connie

I quickly grabbed my phone to call LC. She had been a no-show at work and had been unreachable by phone lately. The last time I spoke with Connie, she told me LC was planning to make things right with her father. The only thing I knew about

THE DREAM LIFE

her father was that he had once lived in America but was deported to Sicily after getting involved in many criminal activities.

I decided to follow the note's instructions and go to her house. She lived in Woodstock, and the traffic was terrible, so it took the Uber over two hours to arrive. The place looked abandoned. Her grass was overgrown, and not a soul was in sight. I rang the doorbell for what felt like forever, but no one answered.

"What in the actual hell is going on around here?" I said aloud, going to retrieve my spare key from its hiding spot, but I couldn't find it there. To my dismay, I remembered I hadn't put the hideaway key back when I was here last. I checked every point of entry I knew of, but everything, even the hidden cellar, was locked.

I went back to the door and knocked, as if I were a police officer. Still, no one answered. I sat on the porch swing and tried to figure out how I could get in without breaking a window. I decided to call the real police. I would tell them my sick relative had been unresponsive for days and I needed to get inside to check on them. As the phone rang, I heard a siren in the distance. The dispatcher said, "9-1-1, please hold." The siren's sound grew louder and louder. I saw the lights coming down her long driveway not too long after.

The paramedics quickly sprang into action, pulling out the gurney.

"Did you call 9-1-1?"

"Ugh. Yes, but I'm still on hold and haven't spoken to anyone yet. Why are you all here?"

"We got dispatched here. Someone at this residence was reportedly unresponsive. Where is the person, ma'am?" I was thrown off by how quickly they had arrived. But I hadn't spoken to anyone or given any info yet. Did Siri send them? I was so confused.

"I'm sorry, but my friend lives here. I've been knocking, and no one has answered the door yet. Are you sure you're at the correct address? I haven't even spoken to the dispatcher yet."

"Is this 819 Oak Bluff Lane?"

"Yes, it is. But…"

"Ma'am, I'm sorry, but seconds wasted on this job could mean life and death. Now, is the person who lives here alone?"

"I'm not sure. As I said, I've been out here trying to understand myself. I got a note from Connie saying to come…." My stomach started feeling weak as I grew nervous, wondering what might be happening inside. Is LC okay? Is Connie hurt? I lost my balance a bit as panic began to take over my mind.

"Ma'am, ma'am…" The paramedic shouted, grabbing my arm to steady me.

"Are you okay, ma'am?"

"Yes, I'm sorry. My head suddenly feels dizzy. I'm still healing from a head injury."

"Could you tell me your name?"

"Rae," I said, short of breath.

"Rae, I'm Whitney. Let's walk over here and have a seat. That's right. Everything is going to be just fine," she said in a reassuring southern accent as she guided me to a spot to sit down.

  THE DREAM LIFE

Her partner returned. "Whitney, all the doors are locked. The shades are drawn, so I couldn't see if anyone was inside the house from the outside. We're probably going to have to break in. I'll call the chief for permission." The young man radioed his superior with the update, and permission was granted.

As they hurried inside, I stayed still on the porch, feeling like I was glued to the seat. I felt like I was in a dream, and life no longer felt real or made complete sense. My breathing became shallow. "Please be dreaming," I whispered aloud, closing my eyes as if I was making a birthday wish. The anxiety was taking over, so I decided to rest my head between my knees and breathe deeply. The technique seemed to be working because I sensed my thoughts calming down. When I finally stood up to enter the house, the paramedic almost ran me over with Connie on the gurney. He was administering oxygen to her through a bag valve mask.

"Connie!" I screamed. "What happened? Where's LC?"

"What happened?" I frantically demanded to know from the paramedic.

"Ma'am, all I can tell you right now is she still has a heartbeat. I need you to listen to me, ma'am. Ma'am!" he screamed, bringing me out of my hazy daze.

"Yes, what can I help with?"

"Come get the AED and take it to my partner STAT!"

I ran into the house after he handed me the AED.

"Whitney! Where are you?" I shouted, running to each room, trying to find her location. The moment felt unreal, like when you're running away from a monster in your dream and your feet cannot move fast enough to get away. It felt like time was warped. I begin to hear her faint voice saying, "Rae …" repeatedly.

Room after room, I still couldn't find her inside the vast estate. As I returned toward the front of the house, I saw that the basement door was open.

"Whitney?"

"Rae, down here." Her voice called out, sounding closer now. I rushed down the staircase as fast as I could—or at least it felt that way. My mind wasn't ready for what I saw. Whitney's face was pale with a grayish hue as she poured everything into performing CPR on LC's lifeless body.

"LC!" I fell to her side and grabbed her hand. Whitney set up the AED and said, "Stand back, Rae." The first dose of electrical current didn't revive her. Whitney paused for a moment, then administered another shock.

"LC, wake up, please! LC, it's me, Rae! Get up, please!"

   THE DREAM LIFE

CHAPTER 27

"Deep into that darkness
peering, long I stood there, wondering,
fearing, doubting, dreaming dreams no
mortal ever dared to dream before."

- Edgar Allen Poe

The hospital waiting room was lively that evening. One group of family members was huddled together on their knees, praying for a miracle. Another family was already at each other's throats about their grandfather's inheritance, whom the doctors hadn't even pronounced dead yet. Connie's family was occupying a section of their own. Every seat seemed to have a soul sitting and waiting for an outcome. I decided to walk to the gift shop in hopes that the outcome for LC and Connie would be positive. When I called Jessie to give her the news about my whereabouts and what had happened, she said she would be on her way as soon as possible to drop off some items for me. She knew I wasn't going to leave LC's side. Of course, I couldn't. LC had been like a second mom to me, and I wasn't going anywhere. The waiting was driving me up the wall. I was trying to piece together a theory of what I thought had happened behind those doors at LC's estate. LC didn't have a pulse. Connie did, but she was unresponsive. What could have happened?

Another hour passed without a single doctor coming out to give any of us waiting souls an update about our loved ones behind those doors. It was agony. Half of Connie's family had already left, so I was there trying to comfort her son and daughters with my limited Spanish vocabulary. "¿Por qué Ms. Rae?

¿Qué pasó?" they continued to ask me, but I didn't know what to tell them.

When the doctor finally came through the door, she was bombarded by groups of families. "Ramirez. Are any of you related to Connie Ramirez?" Connie's family charged toward the doctor.

"Ms. Ramirez is in stable condition now. She seems to have sustained an episode of myocardial ischemia. We are doing all we can to ensure her prognosis doesn't worsen, so she will have to stay with us until she's cleared to go home. You

          THE DREAM LIFE

all can see her now." I stayed in tow with Connie's family to get behind those doors to find out what was going on with LC.

Connie was tubed all over. "¡Mija!" her youngest daughter bellowed as she ran to her mother's bedside. Connie was still out of it, but the nurse said her vitals were good. After receiving the update on Connie, I gave the family my contact information and went to the nurse's desk to inquire about the details of LC's condition. The first question was, "Are you family?"

"Yes, I'm her daughter."

She took her eyes off the computer screen and tipped her glasses on the edge of her nose. "Umph. You're a little dark to be claiming to be her daughter, so you can tell that to someone else. Family only." Her words cut me like a knife, plus I was already on edge, so I snapped at her.

"Listen here, you ignorant heifer. That lady is my mother! I have been in that waiting room for hours to hear an update on her condition. I'm not about to be too nice if I must wait for another second. And I'm sure profiling my skin tone is not in your oath. Take my blood, if that's what's necessary, but I want an update, now!"

"Fine, lady, just calm down. She's still in surgery."

"Surgery! Surgery for what?" I demanded to know.

"Oh, I thought you would have known, being her daughter and all," the nurse said, her voice dripping with sarcasm.

"Please, lady! I'm getting tired of being patient with your unprofessionalism. Tell me what is going on with my mother now, before I come across this desk!"

"Ma'am, have a seat before I call security."

As much as I wanted to go off, I swallowed my anger and anxiety and decided to wait as instructed.

Jessie had brought me food and supplies long ago and left to get ready for Pablo's show. I'd had enough of the waiting game. I went back to the nurse's desk, armed with verbal ammunition, prepared to confront little Miss Bigoted Bitch. To my surprise and relief, her shift had ended, and the new nurse was eager to help me. She told me LC had been out of surgery for over an hour now, and I could finally see her. Even though I had been impatiently waiting all this time to see her, I suddenly felt as timid as a bird flying in the rain. I channeled my inner strength and headed for her room. Behind the large door was one of the most formidable and respected women in the photography and film industry. While others would shy away from conflict, she fearlessly jumped, afraid of nothing above or below. She built her empire her way and would live to tell the story. This lady was featured in Forbes many times. She broke every glass ceiling. She employed thousands over the years. She took in this wandering little Brooklyn girl, along with many others, under her wings and cultivated greatness.

Yet today, she was lying in a hospital bed without a soul around. I stood at the door, marveling at the stillness and peace I never, not even one time, was able to catch her in.

"LC, it's Rae. Even though I know you hate mushy items like this, I brought you a teddy bear and a get-well balloon from the gift shop." I walked around the sterile room looking for answers to what had landed her here. I noticed a chart attached to the hospital bed. I quickly grabbed it and started to scan the words. There were no other words on the page that

　　　　THE DREAM LIFE

screamed to me as loudly as 'malignant' and 'stage 4'. I sank to the floor and started crying like a baby.

***

"Miss, excuse me." I was awakened from my slumber by the same kind nurse who told me where I could find LC.

"Good morning. How are you today?"

Trying not to think of the real answer, I said, "I've had better days."

"Well, it looks like your mother is doing well," she said, going about her duties and tending to my pseudo mother.

"Is her doctor available to speak with me? I don't know what is going on or what landed LC…. I meant my mom here yesterday."

"I'm not sure what time he'll be in, but I will check for you," she informed me.

"Okay. When he arrives, please have him contact me," I said, handing her my business card.

"I sure will. Just hit this buzzer if you need anything," she said, then left. I shared funny stories with LC about memories we made over the years to pass the time.

"I bet you don't remember this one. When you broke up with Tate and went on a blind date. The crazy fool roofied you and stole your purse. And when you woke up, you said…."

"Damn, he coulda at least fucked me first," LC said weakly, coming out of her trance state.

"LC! You're awake!"

I went for the nurse button. "Hey, kid. Oh well, I guess the secret's out."

"Secret? What secret? I still don't know what the hell is going on!"

The nurse came back in. "Well, look who's already awake. Ms. Calloway, you are one tough cookie. I can't believe you are awake with all the morphine coursing through your body. But your vitals are looking good, and the doctor will be in to see you all shortly."

After the nurse left the room, I gave LC a scolding look.

"What? Don't start with me, Rae. As you can see, I'm not in the best condition to have you on my bad side." I said nothing, just stared at her until she folded.

"Okay. What is it that you want to know?"

"How long?"

"How long what?"

"Get serious, LC! I was stretched out on a hospital floor, crying myself to sleep last night, so don't even go there. How long?"

"Kid, what the hell does it matter? Time tells the story as destiny would have it, so why should I?"

"What the hell does that even mean?"

"I don't know. I'm just trying to sound prolific to lighten the mood."

"Did you go to Sicily?"

"Yes."

"Did you see your father?"

"No. I was too late."

"LC, you've always been like a mother to me. You took me under your wing when I was young. What made you think you couldn't share this with me?

"Rae, you know I've always hated mushy, sensitive topics. So, when I got the news, I decided to bury it deep inside. There's not much you can do when you get the news that you're terminally ill."

"Yes, it is. You can fight it."

"Aww, kid, my fighting days are gone. I decided to let my fate come as it may."

"You still have so much life ahead, LC. I believe there's still hope with all these advanced treatments nowadays. I'll be here for you every step of the way. Please, let's fight this thing…"

"No!" she barked, interrupting my plea.

"But…"

"But nothing. This is my fate. This is my time. I ran out of time to make things right with my father. Now I must make things right with you. Rae, the LC company is yours now. Rebrand it. Rename it. Whatever your vision is. Make it your own. It's your time, kid. You are the closest thing I've ever had to having my own child. Looking back now, I realize that you have always been the pathway to my lasting legacy. My protégé. You are my beneficiary, Rae…"

"LC, LC, please stop talking like you are about to meet your Maker. You're not going anywhere, lady." I said firmly. Then I witnessed something that I thought I would never see. LC began to cry.

"Listen, I cried enough last night for both of us. There's no need for you to get upset now, after everything you've been through. Let's change the subject. I'm going to get some coffee and check on Connie."

"Connie? Where's Connie?"

"Oh yeah, I forgot you don't know. You and Connie were both admitted yesterday. The doctors think she had some kind of weird heart thing, but they are still running tests."

After she heard the news, LC started breaking down like a baby. I gently hugged her and told her Connie was doing just fine. She told me to phone her room so she could speak with her, but I suggested that I go to her room first to make sure she was awake.

When I arrived at Connie's room, she was also awake. Her daughter told me that the doctor said her tests confirmed she had a heart attack. Luckily, the paramedics brought her in quickly enough that there was no permanent damage. "Hey, Ms. Connie. How are you feeling?"

"Glad to be alive, Ms. Rae. How's Ms. Calloway?"

"She's awake. I haven't talked to her doctor yet, but she seems okay. She wanted me to call your room, but I wasn't sure if you were awake yet."

"Tell her I will be good, but she makes me worry about her. That's why I'm here."

"Do you remember what happened?" I asked, hoping she could shed some light on this mystery.

"I remember finding Ms. Calloway on the floor. I was so worried, Ms. Rae. I thought she was dead," Connie said shakily, tearing up as she shared her recollection.

"I called 911. And that's all I can remember." Her daughter took a tissue and softly wiped her tears.

"I got your note and came to the house but couldn't get in. When the ambulance pulled up, I didn't know what to think. Well, I'm just thankful you two are doing better. I'll check in on you later. LC's room number is 1110. Call me if you need anything. See you all later."

When I got back to LC's room, the doctor was there, going over treatment options with her.

"I know what your previous physician told you, but the good news is that there's still hope with modern medicine. I never tell my patients they are terminal because I am not God. No one controls your departure. I've seen patients who outlived some doctors who predicted a bleak future. Now, if we can get you transferred to a specialist to start radiation..."

"Thank you, but no thank you, doc. During my many, none of your damn business years on Mother Earth, I made my mark, gatdammit! Not one person alive or dead can say otherwise. Hell, sometimes I feel like I've lived twice. It's been such a thrilling ride. I thank you for the care you've shown me, but I will not need a specialist for radiation."

"LC! Please don't do this. We can fight this thing together. Fuck cancer! Don't leave us. We need you. Please," I cried out to her.

"Rae, I love you, kid, but you don't need me. I've shown you the blueprint. Now it's your turn to handle business. Hell, you're the reason the LC company has grown so much. You got this, kid. It's time for me to step aside."

I grabbed her hand and peered deep into her eyes and whispered, "I need you, LC. Please fight…. please don't leave me."

"I will give you all some privacy. I'll be back later to talk with you about a game plan, Ms. Calloway," the doctor said as if he could change her mind. The truth was, no one could. She was as stubborn as an ox. I rested my head in her lap and silently began to weep. She ran her fingers through my curls.

"Ti amerò per sempre, Rae, ma è il mio momento," she whispered in her lovely native tongue.

"I'll love you forever, too, Lorinza Cavallaro," I declared, using her birth-given name as I wept, sad beyond measure.

CHAPTER 28

Sweet dreams, L.C.

"When you think life has just about depleted you and given you all you can take, that's when a ray of sunshine peaks through the clouds to remind you the storm doesn't last forever," Jessie said, trying to give me a dose of positivity. "Thank you, J. That was beautifully said," I murmured, speaking with my face planted in the cushions of the couch. My vibration was at an all-time low from all the turmoil. Days had gone by, and I couldn't find my way outside my condo or my gloom. I couldn't even bring myself to walk into work knowing LC wasn't going to be there anymore to bust through my office door at any given time.

"Now, about getting back on the road with the crew to get your mind off all this sorrow?" She left the question floating in the air. I sat up to give her my attention.

"Umm huh, go on."

"You know it's about time to finish your contractual duties with Pablo. By the way, they haven't stopped praising the fantastic job you've done so far. And let me tell you, as his fans and sponsors have grown, it might be wise to renew your contract with some additional terms. I can handle that for you if you'd like," she suggested.

"J, of course, I will finish the deals and obligations I signed off on. After that, it's a wrap. I need a reset. A fresh start. A new location. I've been thinking about moving to one of the blue zones. Enough already with these ill experiences. I'm ready to live for me and only me. It's time for me to do something new."

"Like?"

I moved closer to the ceiling-to-floor windows and thought about the answer as I watched the traffic accumulate.

"Hello? Like, what G?" she asked again, interrupting my daydream.

"Well, photography is my passion, so maybe something in that area but different from shooting for the industry limelight. Maybe I'll start my own film and photography school. I can teach these young people how the pros land big contract gigs, just like LC taught me. Or I could start my own production company, build a team, and make some indie films. I don't know, something like that." I walked away from the window and plopped face-down again on the couch.

"Genie, I thought you knew by now… once you get a taste of this lifestyle, you can never truly part ways with it. It's just like being married to the mob. There is no out. True, you can start over in a new city and with a new job, but why would you want to leave these connections, namesake, and money on the table? You want to start your own? Why not do it with a celebrity and a team that pays you a healthy percentage? Whether you or your employees are on set, you can still get paid and do whatever your heart desires."

"Truth be told, I don't care about the money anymore, J."

"Wait. What? Are you having another migraine or a head contusion?"

"No, I'm fine. I realized that all these years of busting my ass and stacking my chips, I still come home to an empty nest. Although I am grateful for everything I've accomplished, I now see that no amount of money is worth a life spent in regret. I appreciate you looking out for me, but working under Pablo's new label is not what I want," I said, opening up to her like never before.

"Okay, could you at least tell him I begged you to stay and you refused? This man offered to increase my salary if I could convince you to renew your contract. I already knew it wouldn't be easy, but I told him I would try."

"He should increase your salary regardless. You're worth every penny," I said, giving her a small smile.

"He did! It seems like he would stop at nothing to get a chance to have you on his team."

"I'll tell him you gave it your best shot, but it's time for me to write a new chapter."

"Genie, I know it's hard for you right now with all the darkness that's been shadowing your light, but I'm starting to worry..."

"No need," I responded abruptly, interrupting her. "I'm a dreamer who will find my way by moonlight."

"Yeah, yeah, Ms. Wilde. However, you can't just wish for your dreams to happen. You have to work for the dreams you wish for," she lectured me.

"I know, Mom," I muttered, sounding like an annoyed teenager.

"At least visit your therapist so you can get the mental help you need to navigate the healing process appropriately."

"That's not a bad idea. Thanks, girl." She walked over and planted a kiss on my head.

"Love you, Genie."

"Love you more," I answered back.

"Alright, I'm headed to the show now. Call me for anything." Heading towards the foyer, she stopped in her tracks, as if she had forgotten something.

Jessie said, "Genie, remember, the only way out is through."

Chapter 29

My dreams once led me to clarity

"Rae, you have to allow yourself to open your mind completely. The pain, the hurt, and the drama are necessary tools for your healing." I knew everything my therapist told me was the key to unlocking trauma and ultimately healing. But even though I had been seeing her occasionally for a decade, I still couldn't let my guard down with her entirely. Perhaps I wanted to hold on to a piece of inclusivity and not let her in on my true insanity. Even God didn't know half my secrets; I was such a private person.

"Okay, well, it's been three sessions in a row, and as I always tell you, if you want to spend your hard-earned money just to hang out with me, I'm cool with that because I enjoy your company. However, I'd love to help you work through these challenges you're facing. After all, that's what I'm here for."

This was the most uncomfortable I'd ever felt with Dr. Tell. I usually ask to meet over brunch or lunch to keep it casual—as if we were just girlfriends catching up on life. Today, she was insistent on meeting in her office.

Lunchtime had passed, but I'd thought I'd still give it a try. "Have you eaten today? I know this new spot…."

"Let me answer your question with a question. Have you been experiencing any PTSD following your attack?"

"Not that I can recall."

"Have you had changes in your appetite?"

"No."

"Any trouble sleeping, insomnia, or abnormal patterns while dreaming?"

"No, not that I can think of…."

"Well, this could be…."

"Wait. Come to think of it, my dreams have vanished since the attack, which is very odd since I have always been a fervent dreamer. I just now realize that I haven't woken up from a nightmare or an overactive dream in a long time."

"Well, that's a normal prognosis for head trauma," Dr. Tell revealed. "However, I do recall from previous sessions how you would discuss your dreams as if they were…." She paused to rethink her words. "Well, I'll just say they were very vivid and detailed." She stopped talking and walked over to her

Rolodex on her desk. "Ah, yes, I thought I had her information here." She jotted down some information on a notepad and then tore the sheet off. "Rae, I have an idea. Have you ever heard of regression therapy?"

"Doesn't that involve hypnosis?"

"Depending on the methods used, but in most cases, a person is brought to a trance state to retrieve lost memories."

"Wasn't this form of therapy labeled as non-accredited?"

"That's only if the therapist is unprofessional and implants his or her own false concepts while practicing this method."

"And what would this do for me exactly? Enable me to go back to that night and see the perpetrators?"

"Only if you can unlock that memory and if you actually saw the attacker's face that night. The head trauma may affect the outcome entirely or not at all."

"So, you would do this at your office?"

"This is not my level of expertise, but I have a colleague critically acclaimed as a phenom for unlocking lost memories to help people heal from past trauma."

"This all sounds like a chapter from an MK Ultra mind control book I once read. Some quack implanting my memories to become a sex slave, assassin, or some shit..."

"Trust me, Rae. I wouldn't have suggested it to you if I didn't believe it would be helpful. The efficacy is only challenged because, as I stated, some hypnotherapists may have unintentionally or intentionally influenced the results or implanted fake truths. However, the real truth always reveals itself when we confront the shadows that reside within us. I encourage you to give it a try."

"You know, Dr. Tell, I've never considered myself someone who's susceptible to hypnosis. I usually let my dreams guide me to clarity."

"Over the years I have known you, I would have to say, I agree with you. However, what do you have to lose by giving it a try?"

CHAPTER 30

> *"I dreamed I was a butterfly, flitting around in the sky; then I awoke. Now I wonder: Am I a man who dreamt of being a butterfly, or am I a butterfly dreaming that I am a man?"*
>
> *—Zhuangzi*

"Now, what do you see, Rae?"

"Darkness. I see darkness."

"Take a deep breath and unlock your senses. Can you pick up on any smells?"

"Umm, eucalyptus, sandalwood…wait. Is that a Nag Champa incense I smell burning?"

"Okay, now go deeper into your senses from that night."

"Sorry, doc, but how am I supposed to tap into a smell from a night that I'm not in? Numerous other scents are permeating this current atmosphere. Time travel?"

"Yes, time travel in your memory. Take a deep breath, hold it…let it out…and relax from the tip of your head to the soles of your feet. Become aware of all your senses. Melt. Breathe. Hold it. Let it go. Melt. Breathe. Hold it. Let it go…."

This was my fourth session with the phenom Dr. Pamela, and let's just say she hadn't been successful at unlocking my memories. I don't know if it was my reluctance or stubbornness that was interfering with my ability to enter the trance state that she wanted me to reach.

"Ms. Roman, this is our fourth attempt, and I am genuinely amazed by your inability to achieve complete suggestibility."

"Don't be, Doc. I told Dr. Tell I didn't think this was a good option for me."

"Well, don't throw your hat in just yet. I have an idea that just might do the trick. But…"

"Oh no, not a 'but'. Please don't say hallucinogenics." "Oh, great, you said it, so now I don't have to." She laughed. I didn't.

"Are you serious right now?"

"Yes, I am. Using an aid to give you a break from overthinking will help you relax."

     THE DREAM LIFE

"Oh wow, she's serious," I said in disbelief and proceeded to gather my belongings to exit this quack's door.

"Wait. Where are you going?" She stood and walked toward the door.

"It's bad enough that you're trying to control my thoughts, and now you want to dose me too? I'm out of here!"

"First, I'm not trying to dose you. Second, as the patient, you have to agree and sign a waiver agreeing to drink the tea."

"Okay, I'm getting serious Jim Jones vibes now. It's time for me to get out," I said, making finger quotation marks, then pushed past her.

"Ms. Roman, please. Wait. Can you please…"

As I waited for my Uber, I phoned Dr. Tell to give her a piece of my mind for referring me to this unorthodox quack. She informed me that dosing a patient is not as bizarre as I had understood for this type of therapy, especially when the patient is not allowing themselves to fall into a hypnotic state. She even shared that electroshock can be used as a therapy tool to uncover past trauma and past lives in some cases.

She calmed me down and helped me realize I was overreacting to her suggestion because I feared giving someone else autonomy over me. I returned to Dr. Pamela's office and apologized to her for being irrational and for prejudging a therapy method I knew nothing about.

A week later, I tried it again. Dr. Tell was kind enough to accompany me to the fifth session and drive me home afterward. Dr. Pamela explained that I would be going on a journey using a unique blend of Ayahuasca tea. As I slowly sipped this witch's brew, I started to feel a calming sensation spreading, a tingle through my body. The doctor began to recite her hypnosis jargon. Today, she added a new element: a Tibetan singing bowl and a sleep mask.

"This is to keep your eyes from popping open," she stated, placing the black satin mask over my eyes.

The bowl hummed as she traced its rim. Then, she drew a pattern of three circles on the rim and tapped the side.

She said, "Allow this sound to take you back to that night," repeating the rhythmic vibration.

"Now, when I say awaken, you will be there…."
Following the same repetitive vibration, she said,

"Awaken."
 Suddenly, I felt thrown into an unknown dimension.

"Rae, tell me what you are seeing."

"I'm walking down the street."

"Tell me what you smell."

"Stinky trash."

"Can you see the trash?"

"Yes, it's overflowing out of the garbage can."

"Become aware of the temperature of your skin. Are you hot or cold?"

"I'm cold. I feel wet."

"Why are you cold and wet? Tell me what you see."

"It's raining."

"Look around and tell me what you see."

"I'm holding my phone, looking at eateries."

"Rae, look up! Awaken!"

"Oh no! Oh no!"

"Now, Rae. You see the attackers. Identify them!"

   THE DREAM LIFE

"I can't. It's dark now. Everything is dark. I can't see anything."

"Focus on your breathing. The light is within. The truth is within."

With every affirmation, the bowl chimed. I began to calm down, only to be transported back into the abyss.

"Go deeper into the shadow. You are wet. It's raining. Awaken into that moment." I could hear her voice, but I could not determine where I was. She repeated the bowl chant. I was back on that street, walking in the rain. Not a soul in sight. I looked back down at my phone. When I turned around, I was face-to-face with my attackers. I could see their faces as plain as day, but they were blank. One was tall, and one was short… they were two white males…The hypnotherapist tapped the bowl again and said,

"Awaken! Open your eyes and see! Awaken and unveil the truth. Unlock your truth. Your strength is within. Your power is within. The truth is within. Awaken to the truth, now."

The vibration's sound placed me in an unfamiliar setting. I felt like I was traveling through dark fog. I couldn't discern my surroundings. I closed my eyes and listened.

Beep. Beep. Beep. The sound of a vital machine —my heartbeat, beeping faintly —awakened me. Then, the sounds of an intercom blared, *"Paging Dr. Bussey to the ER. Code Blue. Dr. Bussey to the ER. Code Blue."*

I tried to hold my head up, but my neck was too stiff. I saw Jessie, my mom, my dad, and Will out of the corner of my eye. "You! Why are you here?" I said to Will in a raspy, weak tone.

"Gene Rae! Oh, praise God! Nurse!!! Go get the nurse, James!"

"What is going on? Why am I back in the hospital? Did something happen in the therapy?" I asked my mom, now highly agitated.

"What are you talking about, baby? What therapy?" She had a baffled look on her face. The nurse came into the room. The look on her face was one of astonishment.

"Well, look who is finally back in the game. Wow, this is great news. I'm going to go inform your doctor right away!" She scurried back out the door after checking my vitals.

"Do y'all see what the power of prayer can do?" my mom started. My dad walked over and planted a sweet kiss on my cheek. Jessie was breaking down, crying in the corner. Will was at my side, holding my hand.

"Am I imagining all of this or what?"

"No, my sweets. I can't tell you how happy I am that you are finally awake," Will said passionately.

"Get away from me, cheater," I said, snatching my hand away from his. The words seem to shock him.

"Rae, sweetie…" he said, a hurt look overtaking his features.

"Aht-Aht… Go 'sweetie' that bitch you were screwing in the red thong you bought for me." My statement seemed to jolt everyone in the room.

"Rae, you couldn't possibly…wait a minute. How…I mean… I'm going to step out and see if I can find the doctor."

"When you find the doctor, see if they will prescribe you a pill to keep your dick in your pants!" I tried to shout as he walked out the door, but my voice cracked horribly, and I started to cough.

Jessie snapped out of her sad state and hurried over with a bottle of water. "Hey, best friend. Girl, you just don't know. I'm so happy to have you back to consciousness again! I have missed you terribly, and I have many things to fill you in on…." My mom stepped in and interrupted Jessie's rant.

"Let my daughter take a moment to breathe so we don't set her back," she said sternly, giving Jessie an unusual side-eye look. "Gene Rae…I have prayed around the clock that God would take charge, and finally…" she paused for the dramatics, dabbing the corner of her eyes with the embroidered handkerchief my dad gave her as a 25th wedding anniversary gift.

I closed my eyes and opened them repeatedly until I was brought back to reality, or at least what I thought reality was. However, what I saw before me was undeniably tangible and real. How could this be? *Damn, this tea has me tripping*, I thought.

"Can one of you please tell me where I am? Where's Dr. Houdini?"

"Who's Dr. Houdini, Babygirl?" my dad asked, scratching his right temple. "What's taking that doctor?" he muttered, looking toward the door.

"Well, baby, something terrible has happened to you. Gene Rae, some evil men attacked you," my mom gently stated.

"Who were the men? Identify them…" I repeated the phrase that replayed in my subconscious.

"They were some good-for-nothing men who worked at your company. Will had detectives working around the clock until they finally got them. It took a while, but we just got the news this week. And yes, they are in jail. Praise God! I'm so sorry they savagely put your life in such peril, Gene Rae. Oh, and baby, I have some sad news to deliver. Your boss, LC…."

"Wait!" I put my hands on my temples to massage the absurd notions away, but a tender feeling was wrapped behind what felt like bandages.

"Mom, why are you telling me information I already know? I know I was attacked. I just saw their blank faces in the fifth regression session with Dr. Pamela. I already know that LC passed away."

"What! Passed? That lady was alive last time I checked, but she's not doing too good with the cancer and all."

"LC's alive?! How? I watched her take her last breath with my own two eyes!"

"You must have dreamed that, baby. After all, you've been resting for some time now. The doctors said 'coma'. I told them you are just resting. That's all. My baby just needed some good rest. That's what I would say to them. You did, however, experience many seizures while resting, but your strength and God brought you through it all. Praise Yahweh! Besides that, the staff here has been so thoughtful and kind to James and me. They've taken such great care of you after your attack."

"Dad, please tell me the truth. Am I tripping on the Ayahuasca? What's happening to me, Dad? Is LC indeed alive?"

"Yes, honey, she's alive. But she's been going through it. She was an absolute mess when she received the news about

     THE DREAM LIFE

you being in a coma. She calls almost every day to see if you have awakened. The last time I took her the care package your mama made, the housekeeper said she was on her way to Sicily to reunite with her father. But she is in fact alive. You must have dreamed that, Babygirl." I looked around the room at my loved ones. They were staring at me as if I had lost my mind.

"So, Will, have you or have you not been sleeping with Cindy?" Will's face displayed embarrassment.

"Rae, you are my soulmate. My angel…"

"No, I need to know the truth now. The last time I remember seeing you, I caught you lying and creeping around. Are you all telling me I've been in a coma for some time and never woke up from the attack until now? Bullshit! I've been living my life. What's happening to me?"

Everyone's eyes were on Will, instead of helping me sort out my realities. He abruptly exited the room.

"I guess that answers your question, Genie," Jessie said.

"I never liked that boy," my mom huffed. "I told you not to get back with him, but you never want to take my advice," my mom began to vent. "You are lying here half-dead, and he's out here getting his freak on? I knew it. Nobody has to work that many damn hours. Oops, forgive me, Lord." My mom suddenly stopped ranting as if she had bitten her tongue and asked me, "But baby, how did you know that?"

"I lived it in my dreams. I can't believe this. Has it all been a dream? Everything?" I asked in disbelief.

"It was all a dream, Babygirl. Now it's time to wake up. I knew the mountainous spirit you carry within would soon awaken," my dad said, holding my right hand. My mom held my left hand. Jessie was at my feet. I looked at them as if they were body snatchers. They also stared at me strangely.

I felt like an alien inhabiting my own body, overwhelmed with disbelief. It seemed I had been living in a parallel universe and had somehow slipped back into reality. After a few breaths to regain composure, I clearly understood the lesson I needed to take from this experience.

They watched me silently, waiting to see what I would reveal next.

I said to them, "I am Everest. All weapons formed against me shall make me prosper."

ACKNOWLEDGMENTS

To my husband—whose steadfast support and love give life to my dreams, thank you for walking beside me through every chapter.

To my parents—thank you for showing me every definition of love and always supporting my dreams.

To my mothers, grandmothers, aunties, sisters, girl-cousins, and girlfriends—each of you is a living testament to the beauty and complexity of womanhood. My circle is powerful because of you. Thank you.

To my incredible family, friends, and supporters—thank you for your constant love and inspiration. I couldn't have done this without you.

To C.T., you taught us to read, to imagine, to see,
To write our own stories, to set our words free.
You lit the spark when others passed me by,
You noticed my passion and urged it to fly.

You guided my path towards the literature road,
With semantics and persistence, you quietly sowed.
Now the seeds you planted have grown even farther…
Thanks to you, I'm a published author.

Photograph by Kristien King

Gene Rae Roman developed a passion for the arts and literature early in life. She first gained recognition for her writing when she entered and won a contest with a fictional thriller about flesh-eating pumpkins on Halloween night.
In her debut novel, *The Dream Life*, she explores nonlinear paths that weave mysteries around life and romance. When she's not robotically existing in The Matrix, she's radiating self-authenticity, basking in creativity, digesting old and new cultural phases, visiting new sights, dancing in the moonlight, and gathering notes for
a new story to tell.

www.ingramcontent.com/pod-product-compliance
Lightning Source LLC
Chambersburg PA
CBHW060301310726
48976CB00007B/2163